"From conception to birth is nine months...."

Though Steele's snide comment made Ravelle wince inwardly, she tried bluffing her way out. "Yes, well, isn't that clever of you to know. But I fail to see what your observation has to—to do with me."

"Your daughter's date of birth—kindly provided by your fiancé—just about coincides *to the day* with conception having taken place that last night aboard the *Capricornia*, Ravelle!" he explained harshly.

"You think Sam might be *your* child?" she half laughed on a hollow breaking note. "Th-that's r-ridiculous! She was—she was born a month prematurely!"

"You lying little witch!" Steele exploded savagely. "Do you really expect me to believe that?"

"I don't care what you believe! Samara isn't yours!" she cried almost hysterically. "Leave me alone! I hate you!"

KERRY ALLYNE

coral cay

Harlequin Books

TORONTO • LONDON • LOS ANGELES • AMSTERDAM
SYDNEY • HAMBURG • PARIS • STOCKHOLM • ATHENS • TOKYO

Harlequin Presents edition published July 1982
ISBN 0-373-10513-4

Original hardcover edition published in 1981
by Mills & Boon Limited

CHAPTER ONE

RAVELLE FENTON stood at the rail of the large powered catamaran as the twin islands of Morning Retreat at last appeared on the horizon. It had been a two-hour trip from the Queensland mainland to the Barrier Reef resort, and her dark brown eyes drank in the beauty of the scene appreciatively on seeing those white-fringed oases of green emerging from the sparkling, azure-coloured sea.

One island—Hermitage—was considerably larger than the other and obviously of continental origin, its hilly slopes covered with pine trees, its beaches boulder-strewn. The other—Hideway—joined to it at low tide by a causeway created from reef growth and sand, was a true coral cay and although its vegetation was no less dense, it was of a typically tropical nature. Graceful coconut palms—originally planted the previous century on many of the islands by the government as a form of sustenance for those unfortunate enough to be ship-wrecked along the two thousand kilometres of beautiful but treacherous reef—swayed gently above dazzling white sands, interspersed with prop-rooted pandanus and finely fronded casuarinas, the ground beneath covered with the spreading, shapely leaved silver tourne-fortia. Farther inland, shading the various community buildings and cabins barely visible from the sea, the tops of tall pisonia trees could be seen, their roots providing a haven for the burrows of the ubiquitous mutton birds.

From the beach a long wooden jetty stepped out through the inviting yellow-green waters of the reef-

5

enclosed lagoon towards the deeper blue of the navigation channel, a tall-masted yacht and a canopied cabin cruiser moored alongside, their shiny white hulls reflecting brilliant flashes of light from the sun-drenched sea.

A change in the catamaran's direction as they prepared to make their way through the narrow opening in the coral had the soft sea breeze ruffling long strands of golden hair across Ravelle's cheek and she combed them back into place with slender fingers as she turned to the man beside her, her wing-shaped brows lowering sympathetically.

'How do you feel now?' she asked in a pleasantly husky voice. Surprisingly, since in her estimation it had been a remarkably smooth trip, her fiancé, Matthew Inglis, had complained of feeling unwell from almost immediately the time they had pulled away from the wharf on the mainland.

'Not much better,' he answered sourly, and swept his hand over a decidedly pale and clammy-looking forehead. 'I shall be glad to get off this damned thing! You know I've never been particularly fond of boats, or the sea for that matter.'

'I'm sorry,' she apologised quietly, self-deprecatingly, and returned her attention—somewhat unseeing this time—to the scene before them.

When she had suggested Morning Retreat as the venue for their last holiday prior to settling down to hard saving before their marriage he had mentioned no such aversion then, she recalled a little resentfully. In fact, she had been quite amazed at the docility with which he went along with the idea. He usually liked to be the instigator of all their plans. Now she was beginning to wonder if she had done the right thing, after all. If things weren't to his liking, Matthew could, on occasion, be a very depressing companion, she knew from past experience.

A slight bump as the vessel came to rest against the piers of the jetty roused Ravelle from her introspective thoughts, and once the mooring ropes had been quickly secured the passengers began heading for the lowering gangplank. There was a crowd of people of assorted ages waiting on the jetty—holidaymakers about to return to the mainland—and while one of the crew assisted the incoming visitors ashore, another two efficiently offloaded their luggage on to a trolley ready to be towed to the resort by a mini-moke.

On reaching the top of the wharf Ravelle could feel the sun beating down fiercely, bitingly, on to the skin of her back and shoulders bared by the strapless cotton sunfrock she was wearing, and she smiled expressively.

'It's lovely and warm, isn't it?' she commented happily. At home, down south, they had still been experiencing cooler spring conditions.

Matthew's acknowledging expression was more of a grimace. 'Too warm!' he retorted with undisguised feeling, hazel eyes squinting against the glare. 'So don't let's waste any time getting into some shade, eh? I could do with a drink now that I'm off that wallowing barge.' He promptly began making for the island with rapid strides.

Although she privately considered his remarks concerning the catamaran to have been rather exaggerated, Ravelle said nothing, but kept pace with him as best she could over the spaced planks in her high-heeled sandals. As he obviously hadn't travelled well, she made allowances for the fact that he was probably still feeling a bit under the weather and it was manifesting itself in his current show of somewhat peevish behaviour.

All along the jetty there were notices prohibiting fishing in the lagoon, and on gazing down into the crystal clear water Ravelle could imagine how they must have brought groans of anguish to the throats of many keen anglers, for there were schools of brightly coloured fish, both large and small, darting around the piles of the wharf and among the masses of coral so plainly visible from that height above the pellucid sea.

'I bet you'd be willing to put up with the heat if you could just dangle a fishing line in there,' she teased in an effort to put her fiancé in a better frame of mind. If there was one thing Matthew *did* like, it was fishing.

'Huh!' he snorted, disgruntled. 'There's not much hope of what with all these *No Fishing* signs around, is there?'

'Maybe not here, but I believe they frequently arrange fishing trips for the guests to the outer reef,' she offered encouragingly.

'By boat!' He sent her a speaking glance.

Ravelle's lips twisted ruefully. She hadn't thought of that. But now that he had reminded her, whenever they had gone fishing before it had always been from a breakwater, or the beach, or in a river. Never away from dry land.

'Well—perhaps, if you took some travel sickness pills you'd be okay,' she proposed helpfully. 'It does seem a pity, though, to come to an area recognised as one of, if not *the* best fishing spot in the world, and not try your luck.'

'Hmm,' he pondered speculatively, and giving her cause to hope his querulous mood might have been lifting. 'I'll think about it. I don't want to rush into anything.'

'No, of course not,' she agreed, averting her face in order to hide the wry tilt which caught at her soft lips.

Not once during the two years she had known him, had she been aware of Matthew making an undeliberated move. Impulse was usually non-existent in his rather discriminatory character, and everything was carefully measured for effect before he would ever commit himself to any course of action. At times the overcriticalness inherent in his nature would grate unbearably on her nerves, but then she would purposely remind herself of some of his other traits, reliability and guilelessness—so different from those she had encountered on her last heartbreaking holiday four years ago—and she would start to count her blessings instead of finding fault.

At the end of the wharf a sandy patch snaked between rustling palms and lacy-leaved tree ferns, providing Matthew with the shade he desired, and leading the way towards the thatch-roofed reception and restaurant buildings where multi-coloured bougainvilleas spilt their magnificent blooms over verandahs and latticed trellises.

With so many guests arriving at the one time the reception area was rather chaotic for a while, but the auburn-haired young woman behind the counter had obviously handled the same situation on numerous other occasions and lost none of her relaxed poise as she sorted out accommodation arrangements and varying enquiries with equal efficiency and friendliness.

Because most of the island's cabins were twin or family units, Ravelle and Matthew found their allotted single lodges were quite some distance apart. Hers, not far from the large round swimming pool, close to the beachfront and the causeway; his, farther back among the trees, along one of the marked walking tracks.

'I thought we'd at least be a bit closer together,' he complained after they had viewed his accommodation and then made their way to hers.

'Perhaps we should have shared,' she joked. 'It would have been a lot cheaper, if nothing else.'

Matthew looked shocked, his prudish upbringing asserting itself. 'An expense I would rather pay than indulge in promiscuous behaviour,' he declared righteously. 'I'm surprised you would even consider it, knowing my feelings concerning such matters.'

'Don't worry, I meant the room, not the bed,' she revealed drily.

All the same, it did make her wonder, and not for the first time, if she was being entirely fair, in view of his beliefs, in allowing him to continue thinking she had been married previously, as her parents had always insisted on telling everyone. Their reason, to protect both Ravelle and her young daughter Samara from any hurtful comments which could have been forthcoming if people had known the curly-haired youngster wasn't the product of a youthful marriage, but was in actual fact the illegitimate result of a twenty-year-old's one and only brief contact with the soul-stirring emotion called love. Love! she repeated to herself disparagingly. It may have been that on her part, but as she had very shortly discovered to her despair, it certainly hadn't been on the part of Samara's father!

Thoughts of her daughter brought a wistful look to her face. She had been terribly disappointed on learning that no children under the age of five were allowed at the resort due to the island's remoteness and lack of a resident doctor, and if it hadn't been for her parents' adamant contention that she and Matthew needed some time alone together, she would have cancelled their arrangements immediately. Her fiancé had strongly endorsed her parents' firm stand and, because he was usually very patient with Samara—if a little distant, at times—she had finally given in out of consideration for him.

Now, with a faint smile and a diffident shrug, she surveyed the neat and compact unit—an exact replica of Matthew's except for the colour of the furnishings—with assessing eyes.

'Well, apart from the fact that we seem to be at completely opposite ends of the encampment, what do you think of the place so far?' she enquired.

'Oh, fair, I suppose,' he allowed grudgingly, never one

to enthuse. 'Provided I'm not expected to stay out in that damned sun for too long. There wouldn't be any drink in that fridge, would there?' His brows peaked questioningly as he indicated the small appliance located beneath the laminated breakfast bar. 'I still feel thirsty after that trip out here.'

Bending, Ravelle swung open the enamelled door. 'Mmm, there's lager, draught, export Pilsener, bitter lemon, cola, or orange juice,' she reeled off swiftly.

'I'll have the orange juice, thanks,' he advised, not unexpectedly. Matthew didn't approve of hard drinks, and didn't care for soft ones.

After handing it across, together with a glass from the shelf above the bar, Ravelle poured out the bitter lemon for herself and took a seat on the long-legged stool beside her.

'As lunch won't be on for a while yet, what shall we do in the meantime . . . explore?' she put forward persuasively. The sun beckoned irresistibly outside.

'You can if you like,' he shrugged indifferently. 'I think I'll just unpack and then have a rest. Give my stomach a proper chance to recover, so to speak.'

'It hasn't already?' she frowned, partly in commiseration, partly in surprise. As he hadn't actually been unwell on the boat, she would have thought he'd be over it by now.

'No, it hasn't, as a matter of fact,' he returned irritably, and clearly aggrieved by the sound of amazement in her tone. 'You should know I don't have an overly strong constitution. Unfortunately, it always takes me some time to regain my wellbeing after any upset or illness.'

Only because his mother continually convinced him he was sicker than he really was! At times she treated him as if he was a frail sixty-eight instead of a normally healthy twenty-eight, Ravelle recalled tartly. But knowing it wasn't the type of remark she could make to

Matthew she merely lifted one shoulder in a self-effacing gesture and apologised, 'I'm sorry, I didn't realise the effects would stay with you for so long.'

'No, well, I guess it wasn't altogether your fault,' he was willing to concede, but in a condescending voice. 'After all, you really couldn't understand what it's like having a delicate disposition, could you? I mean, you've hardly had a day's illness since I've known you.'

'I suppose not,' she agreed with a wry half smile. If she had, she certainly hadn't made such a fuss about it as he always did, and neither could she afford to while she had a child to support.

Presently, their drinks finished, Ravelle washed their glasses and returned them to the shelf, despatching the empty containers to the waste bin.

'I'll walk back to your unit with you,' she suggested, searching out her sunglasses and a floppy-brimmed hat as he rose to his feet. 'Then I can follow that track and see where it takes me.'

'Perhaps you'd better take the map with you.' He pointed to the printed pamphlet the receptionist had given them and which detailed the various routes available.

'No, I don't think so,' she shook her head, smiling. 'On an island this size I doubt you could get lost if you tried, and it will be all the more pleasant to come across things by accident rather than being told beforehand what you're going to find.'

'You don't mean to cross over to the other island, then?'

Once again she shook her head negatively. 'I shouldn't think there would be time this morning, and anyway, the tide could be in at the moment for all I know. I didn't really notice whether it was high or low when we came ashore.' Passing through the doorway she sent him a querying glance. 'Did you?'

'Hardly!' he grimaced scornfully, following her. 'By then I'd had quite enough of the sea for one day. I wasn't interested in the slightest in the state of the tide.'

'Well, as it was my original intention to stay within the confines of Hideaway, I may as well keep to that plan. We can leave Hermitage till another day, when we can both go together.'

'As long as you don't expect me to go tramping through kilometres of bush. You know that's never been my idea of a good time.'

'Perhaps we could ride,' she proposed eagerly. 'It said in the travel agent's brochure that they have horses for hire over there.'

Matthew looked at her as if she had gone mad. 'I can't ride!' he expostulated

'Neither can I,' Ravelle laughed unconcernedly. 'But I don't suppose they only cater for experienced riders. They must get a lot of beginners too.'

'Hmm, on old nags that couldn't run out of sight on a dark night, no doubt,' he scoffed

Ravelle fixed him with a long appraising look from beneath the wide brim of her hat. 'Would you want anything more spirited on your first attempt?' she quizzed ironically.

'Probably not,' he shrugged. 'But nor do I want my arms wrenched from their sockets in an effort to keep my mount from returning to its stable. I've heard what these horses are like when they know there's someone inexperienced on their back.'

'Not all of them, surely?' she sighed as they passed the mini-golf course behind the restaurant. So far nothing she'd suggested had found favour in his eyes. 'I mean, if others can manage them, why couldn't we?'

'I didn't say I *wouldn't* be capable of managing it, Ravelle,' he informed her in pompous accents. 'Merely that I didn't wish to make the effort.'

Drawing in a deep breath, she held it to the count of ten, then released it slowly. 'In that case, perhaps you'd be good enough to tell me just what you *are* planning to do while we're here?' she queried with a sarcastic lift to her brows. 'You've already vetoed fishing trips and bush walking. I know from home that you don't particularly like swimming, and as you've done nothing but complain about the sun since you arrived, I presume you're not a likely candidate for the golf, half-court tennis, or reef exploration either! Now you're squashing any ideas regarding riding as well.' She paused momentarily, her lips shaping into a disappointed line. 'Isn't there *anything* here that interests you, Matthew?'

Ignoring her outburst, he pursed his mouth contemplatively as he mulled over her last despairing enquiry. 'Well, I did see they had snooker and table tennis tables in the games room beyond the reception area. I quite enjoy both of those,' he relayed thoughtfully.

'Snooker and table tennis!' she just couldn't help exclaiming in wide-eyed shock. 'You could play those in the work's social club at home in Wollongong! You didn't have to come over three thousand kilometres to get a few games.'

As they reached his cabin he stopped at the bottom of the steps leading on to the porch. 'I'm well aware of that,' he said with a hurt expression. 'However, it wasn't due to any personal wish to visit the Barrier Reef that I agreed to your suggesting we come here, but rather because I knew how much you'd always wanted to come, and what little chance we would have once we were married and saving for our own home.' He cleared his throat selfconsciously. 'Of course, I must admit that Samara's exclusion did play quite a large part in my decision. It meant that you and I would be on our own for the very first time, and I had hoped we could participate in some activities we both enjoyed instead of restricting ourselves to only those suitable for a child's inclusion.'

Ravelle's irritation disappeared as fast as it had arisen. 'Oh, Matthew!' she sighed helplessly. She hadn't realised how constrained Samara's presence had apparently made him feel. 'I'm sorry if I seem to include Sam in too many of our outings—it's just that I have so little time with her, what with being at work all day, that I like to keep her with me as much as possible over the weekends. As for finding an amusement we could both enjoy—well, that's why I suggested we go riding. It was something different to try.'

'But you like snooker and table tennis, don't you?'

'Yes, of course I do, although . . .'

'Well then, there's at least two entertainments we can share,' he broke in complacently, and smiling for the first time that morning. 'Perhaps we could have a game after lunch. I'll meet you at your cabin at twelve-thirty, shall I?'

'All right,' she acquiesced ruefully, resignedly. He was obviously determined she was going to give him a game of one or the other, and if, as he had stated, it had only been for her sake that he had agreed to visit Morning Retreat, then perhaps she owed it to him to go along with what he wanted to do. Besides, she speculated hopefully, if she did play a couple of games with him, maybe he would then be a little more amenable to joining in some of the activities she had been looking forward to, such as snorkelling and reef walking.

It was beautifully peaceful among the overlapping trees on the walking track and Ravelle wandered along unhurriedly, taking in the sights and smells of the lush rain-forest growth, and marvelling at the length of time nature had taken to create such an island paradise. All too soon she found herself passing gnarled and twisted ti-trees as the track led her on to the beach on the seaward

side, where she was suddenly confronted by a broad
vista of the cobalt sea breaking over the reef in gentle
ripples of white foam.

The scene was guaranteed to lure even the most
reluctant of persons to the water's edge and, definitely
not being one of those, Ravelle had her sandals off in no
time at all, crossing the burning sand with swift steps and
smiling pleasurably when the warm waters lapped about
her ankles. Off to her right lay the larger mass of Hermitage, basking beneath the mid-morning sun, and
appearing completely uninhabited except for the tip of a
silver roof she could just espy amid the thick foliage.

Abruptly, the stillness was broken by the totally unexpected lowing of a cow, the sound floating across the
intervening passage with crystal clarity and setting a
grin chasing across Ravelle's curving lips. Now that was
something she hadn't anticipated hearing so far from the
coast and, her curiosity piqued, she turned to her right
in order to keep the island in view as she made her way
leisurely back to the resort.

A few seconds later the cow's call was answered by a
trumpeting bull, but before Ravelle could look up to
scan the wooded hillside for his whereabouts, her attention was caught by a flash of vivid green and blue as a
wrasse came to within centimetres of her foot and she
quickly lost interest in the more mundane creatures on the
other island in her efforts to see what else she might
discover in the warm shallows.

There were shells aplenty—small ring cowries, pointed
creeper shells, sculptured cockle shells, and red-lipped
strombs. A large majority of them still had their tiny
living organisms inside, and after her interested inspec-
tion she replaced them carefully in their sandy resting
places. About a metre from shore a large boulder of coral
played host to a small school of streamlined silver fishes,
while all along the water's edge small pieces of staghorn

coral, broken from the reef by storms, lay waiting to be eroded into particles of dazzling white sand.

Ahead of her, two young boys were snorkelling under the watchful gaze of their sunbaking parents, their movements scattering more of the beautiful wrasses towards Ravelle, together with a couple of small rays, and whetting her appetite for the time when she would be donning goggles and snorkel too. There was so much she wanted to see and do while at Morning Retreat, she wasn't quite sure where to begin.

With a smiling agreement for the sunbaking couple's friendly, 'Morning—lovely day, isn't it?' as she passed them, she continued on towards the resort, hearing the tranquil silence disturbed by the whine of an outboard motor this time. From Hermitage a low-hulled craft began slicing across the narrow channel, its bow wave frothing brightly on either side, the bare-chested man at the tiller a dark mahogany brown.

The boat reached the beach just below the swimming pool only minutes before she did, its occupant tilting the engine inboard and deftly mooring it by thrusting the anchor into firm sand, then heading for the main buildings with supple strides. As his direction would be taking him past her unit Ravelle found herself following in his footsteps, her eyes unconsciously surveying his virile form.

His dark brown hair probably accounted for the richness of his tan, she surmised musingly, but the husky width of his shoulders and back owed their existence to nothing but an extremely powerful stature. The skin about his lithe waist was firm and sleek, his hips lean and limber. Below well-fitting shorts his legs were long and hard, the muscles flexing easily as he walked with a light barefooted tread.

However, to her dismay, and even before her appraisal was completed, it had begun to strike her just how similar the figure in front of her was to that of the man who had caused her so much unhappiness four years before. So incredibly like him, she realised with a start, that of its own volition her breathing had become more shallow and uneven as her scrutiny progressed.

Almost to her unit, Ravelle came to a standstill, the fingers still clutching her sandals tightening uncontrollably about the fragile straps. It couldn't possibly be him, could it? she asked herself tormentedly, not wanting to believe such a coincidence could happen. Fate wouldn't be so unkind as to bring Samara's father and herself face to face now. Not here, while she was with Matthew and there was no escape possible!

From the shadowed beer garden beside the pool the auburn-haired woman who had been in reception suddenly appeared and smiled gaily as she caught sight of him. 'Chantal's in her suite, if that's who you're looking for,' she told him teasingly.

Turning towards her, he presented a good view of his profile to the girl behind him as he laughed and shook his head. 'As a matter of fact it wasn't, it was you or Vance I wanted to see. I came to collect those . . .'

Ravelle didn't hear the last of his words, the rush of pounding blood to her temples preventing her. Oh, God, it *was* Steele! she almost sobbed aloud in her anguish as an icy hand gripped her heart. She would never forget that hard handsome face with those cool grey eyes and shapely mouth. Pictures of him laughing down at her, just as he was doing to the woman beside him, suddenly flashed unbidden into her mind and, pressing a hand to her mouth, she ran for the safety of her cabin on shaking legs.

Inside, she dropped her sandals uncaringly and went straight to her bag to drag out a packet of cigarettes, lighting one hastily and drawing on it with short sharp breaths. Matthew didn't approve of smoking either, but right at the moment he was the last person she was thinking of as she tossed her hat and glasses on to the bed before slumping down beside them. Her thoughts were a chaotic jumble of memories she had never wanted to recall again, but now that the floodgates had been opened there seemed little she could do to stop the waves of painful remembrances from pouring forth, and in the end she had no choice but to accept their presence defeatedly.

She had been twenty when a girl friend and herself had taken a holiday cruise to Japan, but it wasn't until the trip home that she had met Steele Cunningham and his father. At the time they had flown over to that country for some trade commission connected with their pastoral enterprises—they were involved in many forms of real estate, she had later discovered—but owing to the elder Cunningham's dislike of flying had decided to return to Australia by sea.

By the third day out Ravelle had known she was falling in love with the tall, twenty-nine-year-old grazier from outback Queensland, and her happiness knew no bounds because it was obvious, even to the most unobservant, that her feelings were being well and truly returned. The only one to show any displeasure at the situation was Steele's father—a ruthless martinet of a man—but protected by the cocoon of his son's love she had paid no attention to the slighting remarks he made in Steele's absence about her neither fitting in, nor being good enough for his family. As far as she was concerned, the man she loved apparently held no such reservations, and that was all she cared about.

On their last night aboard, the thought of being separated from him on the morrow for the few weeks necessary before he could travel to Wollongong—some eighty-odd kilometres south of Sydney—to meet her family, had her wanting to spend every last minute available in his company, and it had seemed the most natural culmination of their past days together for her to surrender to the desires which had been assailing her to experience the ecstatic fulfilment only his total possession could provide.

It had been the early hours of the next morning before Steele had accompanied her back to her own cabin after her sensuous initiation into the joys of consumated love, but little had she known that the fervently whispered, 'I love you,' she had vowed in parting were to be the last words she spoke to him.

Not very much later the ship had begun docking, and while her girl-friend had gone topside to watch the procedure, Ravelle had stayed in their cabin to complete the packing she should have done the evening before. The ensuing knock on her door which she hurried to answer, believing it to be heralding Steele's arrival, had announced someone entirely different, however. His father.

Even now, four long years afterwards, the memory was capable of sending icy shivers down her spine, because she had instinctively known he wasn't the harbinger of good news. Not with the satisfied smile he had greeted her with, nor the confident way he had walked into the cabin without waiting to be asked.

With a supercilious glance he had silently condemned her less elaborate accommodation, and then reaching into the inside pocket of his superbly tailored jacket, had handed her a folded piece of paper. 'My son has more important matters to attend to at the moment, but he asked me to see that you received this,' he had advised in his most condescending manner.

Accepting it with apprehensive reluctance, she had found it to be a cheque made out in her name and which she had stared at uncomprehendingly. 'I d-don't understand,' she had stammered in reply, shaking her head.

His cold blue eyes had ranged over her scornfully. 'It means, I'm pleased to say, that in the cold light of day, my son realises his filial obligations mean more to him than a one-night tumble at the end of a diverting sea voyage, although it does appear he did consider you were entitled to some compensation for his having,' he gave a short satirical laugh, 'shall we say—misled?—you, and me, into believing he desired a more lasting attachment.' He eyed the paper still held between his fingers meaningfully. 'Very generous compensation too, I might add.'

Ravelle had retaliated in the only way she knew how, with denial. 'You're lying!' she had accused chokingly. 'Steele wants to marry me! He was only saying so again last night. I—I wouldn't put it past you for *you* to have written this out, not him!'

'Oh, no, Miss Fenton.' He had waved her supposition aside with unbearable disdain. 'There was no need for me to do that, I can assure you. My son was more than willing. But if you wish to check my signature against some of my personal papers,' tapping the pocket of his jacket, 'then you're quite welcome to do so, because you'll find there's no similarity whatsoever. As for your comment that Steele said he wanted to marry you— well . . .,' he paused, laughing sardonically again, 'I'm surprised to find someone in this day and age so naïve as not to realise a man is willing to promise all manner of things in order to achieve his own sexual gratification. Promises he has no intention of fulfilling . . . after the event,' he had concluded with mocking amusement.

To this day Ravelle would never forget how she felt at that moment with her world beginning to cave in around her. 'I still don't believe you!' she had refuted his claims doggedly, valiantly, but unable to prevent the seeds of doubt he had sown from springing into inexorable life all the same.

After she'd had a little more time to think on it she

knew that bold writing on the cheque didn't belong to the man eyeing her so disparagingly, because Steele had posted a letter of his father's at one of their ports of call, and the deliberate script thereon in no way resembled the hand which had penned the damning slip of paper she now held. As well as that, she despairingly, embarrassedly, had to remind herself, how else could the elder Cunningham have known of Steele's and her union last night . . . if his son hadn't told him? It wasn't the type of information one would volunteer about an intended wife, but if it was merely a matter of another female conquest, that was something else again.

At that stage, pride, and what little self-respect she had left, was all that had given her the courage to return his gaze unwaveringly. 'Steele isn't like that!' she had insisted, albeit not quite so convincingly now. 'If he wanted to call it quits he'd tell me himself.'

'I think you overestimate your importance in my son's life, Miss Fenton,' had come the taunting, denigrating reply. 'As I said, he has many more worthwhile concerns occupying his thoughts this morning.' Looking through the open porthole, he had smiled pleasurably. 'Not the least of which is . . . greeting his fiancée.'

'F-fiancée?' she had echoed, ashen-faced.

'Mmm, don't you believe me? Perhaps you would care to see for yourself, then?' indicating through the porthole.

On unsteady legs Ravelle had closed the distance between them to stare down at the wharf below. Until that moment she hadn't even realised that the ship had actually docked and the gangplanks been lowered, but the scene which met her eyes and became indelibly etched in her memory soon revealed otherwise.

Steele had just reached the wharf, she saw, when a svelte-looking brunette detached herself from the cheerfully calling crowd and threw her arms about his neck.

What either of them said Ravelle was too far away to hear, but there was no mistaking Steele's action as he bent his dark head to hungrily capture the red lips raised so invitingly to his, or the length of time it took before he eventually released them. Sick at heart, Ravelle felt the sudden sting of hot salty tears at the back of her eyes, her vision hazing painfully, but not before she had noted the rock-sized diamond on the third finger of the sable-coated young woman's left hand.

'You see, I had no reason to lie.' Steele's father had cruelly twisted the sharp blade of agony which was lancing through her. 'I'm merely my son's messenger, carrying out his wishes. While you . . .' those pale blue eyes raked over her mercilessly, 'well, you've certainly been well remunerated for your services, haven't you? So shall we leave it at that, hmm?' And he had started for the door.

'Except for one thing!' Ravelle could remember half crying, half shouting after him. 'You can return *that* to your two-faced son with my compliments, Mr Cunningham!' Crumpling the cheque into a small ball, she threw it at his feet. 'I wouldn't touch his dirty pay-off money! It might remind me who it came from!'

With an expression that was more of a contemptuous smirk than a smile, he had picked it up and pocketed it. 'You may have cause to regret that foolishly impulsive act of grandstanding, although I'm sure Steele isn't likely to complain. *He* knows the advantages of a healthy bank account, even if you don't,' he had mocked as he departed.

After that she had collapsed on to her bunk, sobbing, but once her girl friend had returned and discovered what had occurred, they had left the ship quickly in order to put it, and the memories it evoked, as far as possible behind them.

Sighing, Ravelle moved restlessly on the bed, drew

absently on her cigarette and then stubbed it out, her
thoughts still chained securely to the past.

Of course, at the time she hadn't known she was
pregnant—that thoroughly disturbing realisation hadn't
come till later—but it wasn't until Samara had eventually
been born that she had finally accepted, once and for all,
that Steele was gone from her life for ever. Deep down
she had still been hoping and praying he would contact
her. The only trouble was that as her daughter grew
older and her features became more definitely formed, it
became harder and harder to forget, because Samara
was a true composite of both her parents. She may have
possessed her mother's blonde hair and dainty retrousée
nose, but the darkly framed grey eyes and the lazy
curving of her lips when she smiled were very much her
father's. So much so that, on occasion, it brought involuntary tears to her mother's eyes and a swift stab of
pain to her heart if she didn't deliberately school herself
against it.

Then, two years ago, Ravelle had met Matthew when
she had successfully applied for the position as secretary
to the works manager at the steel foundry where he was
employed as an assistant purchasing officer. Two years
during which their relationship had gradually progressed—his wasn't an extrovert character, and she was
wary of being hurt again—and although he had never
once made her outrageously happy as Steele had, she
could always comfort herself with the knowledge that he
had never caused her such agony of the spirit either.

She didn't love him, but then Matthew didn't seem to
want a highly emotional association. He was shy of, or
embarrassed by, most demonstrations of physical
affection, and it had taken him almost six months before
he had overcome his inhibitions sufficiently to give her a
chaste and somewhat impassive kiss. Not that Ravelle
minded. Most of the other men she had dated since

Samara's birth had either made it plain they didn't want the responsibility of another man's child, or else they assumed that since she was supposedly a widow, she was automatically a merry one. No, it was more a case of companionship which had drawn Matthew and her together, and when he had asked her some weeks previously to marry him, she had accepted as unemotionally as he had proposed.

The only circumstances to have created any doubts in her mind were those surrounding her daughter. At her parents' instigation she had stayed with an aunt in Sydney while awaiting the baby's arrival—giving them time to spread the rumour of her marriage during her absence—and she hadn't returned until Samara was three months old. At the time she had been totally uncaring whether anyone knew of her 'misjudgment'—as her mother tactfully referred to her affair with Steele—but as it had seemed so important to them she had raised no objections.

She had even allowed them to decide that she should refer to herself as Ms Fenton from then on, in the increasingly common trend of married women who didn't wish to alter their surnames. To her it hadn't mattered one way or the other, but recently she had often wondered, as she had earlier that day, if she shouldn't have disclosed the truth to Matthew, or whether matters were best left as they were. It was a hard decision to resolve, but nowhere near as urgent, or as perturbing, as Steele's unexpected appearance on the island, her senses reminded her agitatedly.

Rising to her feet, she crossed to her bag, intending to pull out another cigarette, then, changing her mind, left it to begin pacing about the room, her fingers threading nervously through her shoulder-length hair. If he was also a guest it was inevitable they would meet some time, probably before very long, and the thought had her trembling convulsively. If just knowing he was here could create this amount of turmoil within her, what would she be like if he actually spoke to her, and how could she hide the state of her feelings from Matthew? Or perhaps he wouldn't speak, her mind raced on, brandishing its own kind of hope. After all, the last time he'd had an opportunity to do so he had preferred to send his father to do it for him.

Somehow that recollection helped calm her a little. If anyone should feel selfconscious at their meeting it should be him, she reasoned plausibly. He had been the deceiver, not her! Coming to a halt, she exhaled a decisive sigh. And maybe therein lay her salvation. Surely it was up to her to decide whether they spoke or not, and if she treated him with a show of complete indifference—God, she hoped she could!—then wasn't it more than likely he would steer well clear of her?

CHAPTER TWO

ALWAYS punctual, Matthew arrived at Ravelle's cabin at exactly twelve-thirty to take her to lunch, and assuming a composure she was actually far from feeling she accompanied him to the spacious restaurant which looked out over the pool and the beach.

There were cold meats, salads, and tropical fruit of every description arranged on a long extended table in the middle of the room and, after making their selection, they carried their plates to a smaller table beside one of the glass walls. As soon as they were seated Ravelle understood why there were so few people utilising the dining room, for it seemed that most of the younger guests—in the main, still wearing their swimming costumes—were lunching outdoors beneath the multitude of palms and ferns which shaded the poolside and the beer garden, while only those of an older or more conservative nature—who wished to dress for lunch—were eating inside.

'Would you care for something to drink, sir?' a smiling young waitress stopped next to their table to enquire, her honey-gold skin complemented by the colourful hibiscus-printed sarong she was wearing.

'No, thank you,' Matthew refused rather loftily, and without even a querying look in Ravelle's direction. He gestured towards the carafe already on the table. 'The iced water will be quite sufficient.'

'Well, if you should change your mind, just give me a signal. I'm Jenny,' she relayed in affable fashion before setting off for the next occupied table.

Beyond the glistening pool Ravelle could see the little runabout Steele had used to cross from Hermitage was still at anchor—in truth, it was beached at the moment since the tide had receded considerably in the meantime—and, irresistibly drawn to the tables outside, her pansy brown eyes began scanning those seated at them with a surreptitious gaze.

It didn't take long for her to find who she had subconsciously been searching for, and she swung her glance back to her meal swiftly—only to have it turn back again ungovernably a few minutes later. He was sitting with three others at the edge of the beer garden. One of his companions was the titian-haired receptionist; the other two a tall, well built man of some thirty years, and a petite young woman, perhaps three or four years younger, whose red-gold hair and slight similarity of features, Ravelle suspected, proclaimed some family connection with the receptionist.

From their demeanour it was obvious they were all well known to each other, and when the smaller of the two women leant across to make some smiling aside to Steele, she suddenly wondered if that could be the Chantal the darker redhead had mentioned earlier. Whatever the quip she made, it must have been amusing, because the other three immediately laughed, and so see that undeniably attractive smile on Steele's face once again had Ravelle's pulse abruptly thudding uncomfortably out of control.

'There's no use your keep gazing outside so longingly,' Matthew precipitately reminded her of his presence in arbitrary tones. 'I have no intention of eating my meals where I'm likely to have sand blown in them, or among that rowdy collection of half-dressed individuals.'

'What?' She stared at him confusedly, one word above all others ringing warningly in her brain. Longingly? Oh, surely not! He must have been mistaken. 'That was just interest you saw, Matthew, not longing,' she contradicted determinedly. 'I'm well aware you've never been partial to picnics, or barbecues, or the like, although I hardly think there's any possibility of the sand reaching your food in this light breeze, nor would I call those out there rowdy exactly. They're only laughing and enjoying themselves while on holiday. It is supposed to be a time to relax, you know.'

'Meaning?'

'Only that I think you're exaggerating a little,' she shrugged.

'I see.' His lips pinched together in annoyance. 'So you would rather be eating outside, after all.'

'That wasn't what I said!' With Steele out there? He had to be joking!

'But it was what you meant.'

'No, it wasn't,' she denied, smiling appeasingly. 'I'm quite content to eat in here.'

'Hmm,' he finally allowed himself to be convinced and went on to something else. 'So what did you find while you were exploring? Anything interesting?'

'Well, I discovered the fish are almost tame. I thought one was going to have a nibble at my toes there for a moment,' she chuckled, and grateful for the change in subject. 'Also, I gather there's cattle on Hermitage as well as horses.'

'Oh?' Matthew's voice cooled a little as he handed her one of the glasses of water he'd just poured. 'I thought you said you didn't intend to go over there.'

'Nor did I.' She shook her head in denial. 'Not that I could have done even if I'd wanted to, because the tide was in, but I heard the cattle, I didn't see them.'

He speared a piece of beetroot and chewed on it thoughtfully for a moment. 'Who would they belong to, then? The resort?'

'I wouldn't have any idea,' Ravelle shrugged her ignorance. 'Does it matter?'

'I guess not,' he grimaced, but after a hard-eyed glance round the room muttered something that sounded like, 'Damned capitalists!' under his breath before returning his attention to his meal.

Ravelle didn't bother to comment. Matthew had always hated the idea of someone owning something he could never hope to afford, and from past experience she had found it less of a strain on their relationship if she permitted such denunciations to ride silently.

Instead, she mentioned hopefully, 'The tide's out far enough now for the reef to start showing.'

Matthew lifted his head to cursorily inspect the beach. 'Mmm, so it is.'

'I—er—don't suppose you'd like to take a look at it later, would you?' she enquired tentatively.

'Not particularly. Besides, I thought we'd agreed we were going to play table tennis this afternoon.'

'I was meaning after that,' she explained swiftly. There might still be time before the tide turned.

'During the hottest part of the day?' he disparagingly found another objection.

'It's probably cooler out there with your feet in the water, and you'd get more of a breeze.'

'While still getting sunburnt, and no doubt, sunstroke as well! No, I think I'll give it a miss,' he carelessly destroyed her hopes.

Normally Ravelle would have accepted his decision in good part, but as she knew she was never likely to return to the reef again once they were married, she wasn't going to miss the opportunity to see what she could while she was there.

'You won't mind if I go on my own, then?' she asked in a tight voice.

Momentarily, Matthew's mouth gaped, then he closed it with a snap. 'Not if that's what you would prefer to do,' he granted huffily. 'You just go ahead and enjoy yourself, don't consider me.'

Sensing he was about to work himself up into one of his more difficult moods, she sighed and tried to reassure him. 'Of course, it's not what I prefer, Matthew, but I did ask you if you'd come with me, and you refused.'

'Don't worry about it.' He shook his head, declining to be swayed from his role of neglected companion. 'I expect I shall be able to find something to occupy my time while you're gone, even if it's only reading a book. However,' his meal completed, he dabbed at his lips with a napkin and rose to his feet, 'if you have no objections, I think I'll go and ensure there's a table free for us in the games room . . . before you discover there's something else you would rather do without me!'

'That's grossly unfair!' She twisted round in her seat to censure resentfully at his departing back, and found her attention switching to, becoming riveted by, the tall male figure which lounged negligently against the bar near the doorway.

A figure which began moving steadily towards her and seemed to mesmerise her into remaining where she was like a startled rabbit pinned by a car's headlights, instead of beating a hasty retreat as every instinct she possessed was urging her to do.

'Domestic problems, Ravelle?' a mocking voice tut-tutted.

'I—I . . .' She felt as if she was being choked by her own panicking emotions as she watched Steele leisurely lower himself into the seat Matthew had so recently vacated and, since she didn't appear capable of movement, tried dismissing him instead by warning shakily, 'I d-don't think you're allowed in here d-dressed like that.'

Bare shoulders were flexed indifferently. 'I doubt there'll be any complaints,' he drawled.

As if to prove his point, Jenny, the young sarong-clad waitress, swept past on her way to the bar without a word of reproach for his extremely casual mode of dress, but merely asked in a co-operative tone, 'Can I get you something, Steele?'

'Beer, thanks, Jenny,' he smiled, and caught Ravelle totally by surprise by flicking a questioning brow upwards in her direction. Matthew hadn't even given her a choice previously. 'How about you?' he queried. 'Would you like a drink? Some coffee?'

'Oh—er—not for me, thank you.' Shaking her head rapidly, she thankfully found her legs had regained a life of their own and made to get to her feet. 'M-Matthew will be expecting me.'

'He'll wait!' A brown hand abruptly whipped across the table to latch itself about one of her wrists with a force which made every piece of cutlery and china jump to a jangling tune. As well as Ravelle's nerves. 'Isn't that what husbands always do?'

'Matthew isn't my husband, he's my fiancé,' she

divulged grudgingly, and trying embarrassedly to remove herself from his grip.

'You're wearing a wedding ring,' his reminder flashed back immediately.

She had forgotten how observant he was. 'I'm a—a widow,' she croaked, a bubble of near hysterical laughter lodging in her throat at the thought of what Steele would say if he knew he was her supposedly dead husband.

Jenny arrived with his can of beer, thankfully giving Ravelle a chance to right her breathing, but before the girl could leave Steele had another request to make of her.

'Bring us a glass of wine too, will you, please, Jenny?' he asked.

'White or red?' The waitress looked from one to the other of them in turn.

Since Ravelle had begun to shake her head in a negating action, he answered for her. 'You'd better make it red, I think.' And after she had left, he advised the pale faced girl opposite him wryly, 'You look as if you could use some colour.'

'I wasn't expecting to see you,' she excused her nervousness awkwardly, and eased her chair away from the table slightly when, in order to open his can, he had no option but to release his hold on her.

Tossing the tab into the unused ashtray, he lifted the container in a taunting salute. 'To old times,' he declared in abrasive tones before taking a long swallow. An almost imperceptible movement by her had him fixing her with a cold hard look from eyes the same colour as his name, and a single warning forefinger was pointed towards her. 'And I wouldn't advise you to try walking out on me, or the consequences could prove extremely humiliating!'

With an apprehensive gulp Ravelle subsided on to her chair, knowing full well there was more than a little of his father's relentlessness in him if he cared to display it. In response to Jenny's return with her wine she smiled faintly, winding her slender fingers around the stem of the glass in an attempt to camouflage their trembling. If she'd had her way this meeting would never have taken place, but since Steele had deliberately chosen to acknowledge her presence she seemed to have lost what little control she might have had over the situation.

'So when did your husband die?'

The question, coming out of the blue as it did, took her completely unawares and she unthinkingly gave her stock reply. 'Three and a half years ago.'

His well shaped brows arched explicitly. 'You couldn't have been married for long.'

'I—er—no, we weren't,' she faltered, a flood of colour staining her cheeks as she realised just who she was talking to. 'Only a couple of months, in fact.'

He took another mouthful of his drink. 'Any children?'

'A—a girl.'

'Does she look like you?'

Ravelle dropped her gaze quickly, the waning flush covering her smooth cheeks now flaring into uncontrollable life again. There was no way she could reply to that one while still looking at him. 'P-partly,' she allowed unsteadily.

An unanticipated hint of amusement appeared in the depths of his grey eyes and one corner of his mouth tilted crookedly. 'The way you keep stammering, honey, could give a person reason to believe you feel as guilty as hell about *something*,' he emphasised drily.

'Well, I don't!' Her denial flashed forth vehemently, categorically, and certainly with no sign of shakiness present. God, if anyone should feel guilty it was him! 'It's just that I'm aware Matthew will be wondering what's keeping me.'

To her annoyance he seemed to find something

humerous in that remark too. 'After the manner in which he deserted you, I'm surprised you care,' he mocked. 'In any event, you haven't drunk your wine yet.'

So far she hadn't even started it! 'I don't drink any more. Matthew doesn't approve of liquor,' she informed him tautly.

The sardonic downturn of his mouth revealed all too clearly just what he thought of Matthew's sentiments. 'And whatever receives his disapproval you automatically follow suit like some spiritless halfwit, do you?' He gave a distinctly uncomplimentary laugh. 'You at least used to have a mind of your own, Ravelle.'

For some reason that hurt. Perhaps because Steele's charge was nearer the truth than she would have liked it to have been, she admitted ruefully. Sometimes, she *did* weakly allow Matthew to override her convictions. And if drinking one glass of wine would permit her to escape Steele's nerve-racking presence that much sooner . . .

'All right, just to prove I still make my own decisions,' she shrugged challengingly, and raised her glass to her lips. But in her efforts to show her independence, she too swiftly drank more than she intended, with the result that due to her previous abstinence combined with the heat of the day, she almost immediately found herself feeling quite lightheaded.

Apparently satisfied with the results of his goading, Steele indolently leant farther back in his seat. 'Your fiancé has no objection to providing for your daughter, though, I take it?' he quizzed next.

Ravelle went to shake her head, but on discovering its new-found inclination to roll instead, promptly desisted. 'No, I think he's quite fond of her, actually. Well, at least as fond of her as he would be of any child,' she surprised even herself by confiding.

'That's one hell of a recommendation for a prospective

stepfather, isn't it?' he gibed, looking decidedly un-impressed.

'Oh, I didn't mean it like that,' she protested, trying to redeem her error in having said too much. 'I just meant that—that Matthew doesn't show his feelings easily.'

'He didn't seem to have any trouble in that regard when he stormed out of here.'

'That was different,' she defended quickly, and took another sip of wine. 'I was referring to . . .' she waved one hand in the air vaguely, 'other types of feelings.'

'In other words, he's a cold fish!' Steele surmised contemptuously.

'I didn't say that!'

'Didn't you?' His eyes held hers tauntingly.

'Well, I didn't mean to,' she hunched away from his question uncomfortably. He made her feel she had been disloyal to Matthew, when that hadn't been her intention at all. 'Although I don't know what concern it is of yours, anyway . . . or even why I'm discussing my fiancé with you, if it comes to that.'

'You probably won't be for much longer, so I shouldn't let it bother you,' he drawled wryly over the rim of his can before taking another swallow. 'Because unless I'm very much mistaken, *Matthew*,' with satiric mimickry, 'is about to reclaim his betrothed.'

'Matthew?' she repeated, frowning, and swivelled round to look at the doorway. When she just as rapidly swung back again she was chewing worriedly at her lip. As he strode across the floor towards them her fiancé looked fit to kill!

'In case you've forgotten, Ravelle, I've been waiting for you in the games room!' he burst out irately on reaching the table. 'Or perhaps you've found something else you would rather do, after all!' His eyes flicked pointedly in Steele's direction.

'No, of course I haven't,' she protested hastily. 'And

I'm sorry if I've kept you waiting, but—but . . .'

'Oh, yes, I can see you are,' he cut in sarcastically.
'You could hardly wait until my back was turned
before . . .' He came to a sudden halt, staring at the glass
in front of her. 'And just what's *that* you're drinking?' he
demanded tersely.

'Only a little wine,' she half smiled placatingly, but
seeing the scornful expression edging over Steele's face
she lifted the glass defiantly and downed the last of the
liquid in it. 'See, no more rosé,' she dared to quip
flippantly.

Steele laughed openly, but Matthew wasn't in a
humorous frame of mind and he grabbed her around the
upper arm with hurtful fingers, preparing to haul her
to her feet. 'You're drunk!' he denounced in disgusted
tones.

'Oh, don't be . . .,' was as far as she got before Matthew, in his temper, succeeded in dragging her off her
chair, but causing her to almost fall to the floor in the
process.

'You can't even stand upright!' he accused unfairly.

Abruptly, Steele's muscular form towered over both of
them, his eyes narrowing with dislike as they rested on
the shorter man. 'I think you'd better watch yourself,
feller!' he warned in a rasping voice. '*You* were the
reason Ravelle nearly fell over, not the amount of wine
she's consumed, and just for your future reference . . .
anyone manhandling women on this island finds them-
self back on the mainland in very short order!'

'Is that so?' Matthew's hazel eyes glared haughtily
back. 'Well, in my opinion, they'd do better to keep such
disreputable-looking types as yourself out of the dining
room before they start interfering in matters that are none
of their business! Who are you, anyway, to be telling me
what to do? The local beachcomber . . . or the bouncer?'
he sneered denigratingly.

'Where you're concerned, I guess you could say I'm more than willing to be the latter,' Steele retorted caustically.

'Oh, yes? We'll just see about that! Where's the damned manager?' Catching sight of Jenny behind the bar, Matthew called out to her imperiously. 'You there! Get the manager in here, I want to have a word with him!'

Grateful that at least all but two of the other diners had left, Ravelle tried to restore some sanity to the situation. 'For heaven's sake, Matthew, you're making a scene over nothing!' she exclaimed. 'Can't we please just leave?'

Ignoring her, he barked, '*Now!*' at the girl behind the bar who, after her first surprised glance, had been looking hesitantly at the taller of the two men. With a shrug she now went to do as Matthew ordered.

In the taut silence which followed her departure, Ravelle swung a vexed gaze at each of the men in turn. Steele's was the more composed manner of the two. In fact, as he stood complacently with arms folded across his broad chest, he even appeared to have an amused curve to his mouth, she noted in mounting annoyance. Matthew, on the other hand, had something more closely resembling a fierce scowl on his face, and his figure was held stiffly straight. Sighing, she put out a hand to touch his arm.

'Matthew, I can assure you Steele isn't a beachcomber or a bouncer,' she murmured soothingly. 'As a matter of fact, he's . . .'

'I don't give a damn what he is!' His voice sliced into her attempted explanation savagely. 'Although I notice it certainly didn't take you long to get on first name terms with him, did it?'

'Only because this isn't the first time I've met him.'

'Something you conveniently forgot to tell me about

from your explorations this morning, hmm?' he insinuated nastily.

About to tartly disabuse him of his misconception,
there was no time for Ravelle to do so, for at that moment
Jenny returned with the man Steele had been lunching
with, as well as the redheaded receptionist, who promptly
uttered an aside to him as the two of them continued
across the room. The woman was wearing the same
long, flowing cotton skirt and halter-necked top they had
seen her in last, but from Matthew's point of view,
Ravelle doubted if he was any more satisfied with the
man's shorts and silk knit shirt—or the leather thongs on
his feet—than he had been with Steele's minimal attire.

With only the briefest of quizzical glances at Steele,
the pleasantly good-looking manager smiled and introduced himself. 'My name's Cunningham—Vance Cunningham—Mr Inglis. I believe you've already met my
wife, Erin,' indicating the woman beside him. 'We run
the resort here at Hideaway, and I understand you
wished to see me about something, is that right?' His
light brown brows rose enquiringly.

As she heard the surname, warning bells immediately
began to ring in Ravelle's head, but Matthew had no such
prior knowledge and rushed into the fray, all unaware.

'My oath, that's right!' he confirmed on a grating
note. 'I'd like to know just what sort of a set-up you're
running here when *this* man,' gesturing violently towards Steele, 'contrary to all codes of decency, is permitted to enter the restaurant in such a disgraceful state
of undress, induce my fiancée into drinking liquor against
my wishes, and then have the temerity to threaten me
with removal from the island if I don't conduct myself as
he sees fit!'

Blue eyes aimed an extremely dry look Steele's way,
and then the manager was inclining his head apologetically. 'I'm sorry if your—er—sensibilities have been

offended, Mr Inglis, because we do normally require our guests to dress a little more circumspectly if they intend using the dining room. However, once you've been here for a few days I think you'll find that part of the attraction of Hideaway is the relaxed life-style. At least, that's what our visitors tell us,' he concluded smoothly.

Apparently too smoothly for Matthew, because he promptly fired back, 'Is that all you've got to say? Surely you're at least going to tell him to get himself out of here! And what about his threats and other suspect behaviour? Or is he, for some inexplicable reason, allowed to menace your guests in any manner he chooses?'

'Matthew, please! You've said enough!' inserted Ravelle desperately, cautioningly.

'I'll second that!' From having watched the proceedings with sardonic eyes Steele now entered the altercation on an exasperated note, his arms unfolding and his hands coming to rest on lean hips as he directed the younger man an unmistakable look of aversion. 'Now I'll tell you a thing or two, you ranting little rooster!' he clipped out scathingly. 'One, I rarely come in here at all, let alone dressed like this, but if I do decide to, you can believe me when I say I won't be begging *your* pardon! Two, as far as I'm concerned, it's Ravelle's decision as to whether she drinks a glass or so of wine while she's here, not yours! And three,' he paused significantly, 'you're damned right I'll threaten you if I think it's warranted! People like you we can do without on this island, and I'll tell you what gives me the right to say that too, shall I?' he queried, bitingly sarcastic, and continued without waiting for a reply. 'Well, it just so happens that the Cunningham family—of which I'm a member—owns Morning Retreat, and we take very strong exception to browbeaters like you!'

'No doubt because we won't bow and scrape to every

decree *your* arrogant breed cares to hand out!' sneered
Matthew, undeterred. 'But if you want to issue threats
then I've got one for you too, Cunningham! Keep away
from my fiancée, or I'll really make trouble! That plain
enough for you?'

Hurriedly clearing his throat, Vance stepped into the
breach. 'Look, I think emotions are beginning to run a
little too high around here, so why don't we adjourn to
Erin's and my quarters for a cold drink . . . or a cup of
coffee?' he added quickly, tactfully. 'We really would
like you and your fiancée to enjoy your holiday with us,
Mr Inglis, and perhaps, as you obviously feel we haven't
made a very good start towards that end, if we sat down
to discuss the matter more rationally we could discover
some acceptable manner by which to redress your
grievances.'

Ravelle exhaled a tautly held breath, blessing Vance
for his diplomacy. If anything was capable of putting
Matthew into a more receptive mood, then that kind of
appeal would. The idea that he might have been
receiving favoured treatment when others weren't had
always pleased him.

However, a covert glance from beneath the fringe of
her long silky lashes to see how Steele was reacting to the
proposal, showed him to be half smiling ironically at his
younger brother and, not for the first time, she wondered
why in such a short space of time he should apparently
have come to dislike her fiancé quite so intensely.
Admittedly, this afternoon's efforts hadn't shown Matthew in a particularly endearing light, but then why
should Steele bother to concern himself with her problems? Or was it just the indication of a guilty conscience,
knowing he'd behaved far worse towards her himself?
The thought had her moving closer to Matthew. At least
he would never cause her that much pain!

In the meantime, Matthew was gradually allowing

himself to be appeased—first by Vance's suggestion, and then by Erin as she smiled in a pacifying manner and added, 'Yes, we much prefer to be on good terms with all our visitors, and really, it's such a waste of a holiday to be harbouring any bad feelings.' Just by the easing of his expression it was clear she was making headway and she pressed home her advantage persuasively. 'Perhaps, as a start, you and your fiancée would give us the pleasure of being our guests for dinner this evening?'

'Hmm—yes, I think that would be acceptable . . . as a start,' he granted condescendingly. He wasn't about to be won over too cheaply. 'Provided, of course, that you intend eating inside the restaurant. I strongly dislike being subjected to the whims of nature while I'm dining.'

'Yes, well, if that's what you would prefer,' Vance interposed agreeably, beginning to escort them towards their private rooms behind reception. 'Although, without air-conditioning, we do generally find that it's cooler outside than in during the evenings.'

'Maybe,' conceded Matthew, but disparagingly. 'However, I doubt to such an extent that it would persuade me to eat out there, and especially if no rules regarding dress apply.'

'Oh, I think you'll find it quite different at night,' Vance began, only to have Steele, who was bringing up the rear with Erin, put in drily, 'Perhaps Inglis would rather have all his meals delivered to his unit. That way he wouldn't be called upon to associate with anyone.' And neither would they have to associate with him, the inference was plain.

'No, of course he wouldn't!' This time it was Ravelle who broke in hastily, partly in order to hopefully pre-empt anything Matthew might say, and partly on her own behalf. As her fiancé would no doubt expect her to eat with him, she had no intention of being closeted away from everyone for her meals. 'The dining room's quite satisfactory, even if it does perhaps get a little warm.'

'It could be rather pleasant, just the two of us,' Matthew looked at her to speculate, and either oblivious to Steele's innuendo, or ignoring it in his desire to receive preferential treatment.

'I don't think so,' she grimaced unthinkingly. Then, seeing the tightening look closing in on his face, she realised the full extent of her tactlessness and promptly set about rectifying it by half smiling in a placatory fashion and explaining, 'I mean, not that it wouldn't be nice, just the two of us, but that I'd be inclined to feel I was cut off from—from . . .

'Yes?' he prompted icily.

She had been about to say from what was happening around them, but guessing that would be of no consequence to him, she lifted one shoulder in a defeated movement. 'It doesn't matter. It's your decision,' she sighed.

Mounting the porch, Vance slid open wide glass doors to usher them into a commodious sitting room, comfortably provided with cushioned rattan and lacquered cane furniture, and decorated by a thriving selection of potted ferns and flowers.

'Mmm, I believe I will take up that offer to have our meals in my unit,' Matthew advised Vance once they were seated and Erin had left to make the coffee. He sent Steele, now resting casually in a chair opposite, an extremely pointed glance. 'At least that way I shall know there's no chance of Ravelle being encouraged to drink hard liquor the moment my back's turned.'

Ravelle's fingers clenched nervously in her lap as she waited for the scornful retort which didn't come. To her surprise, and perhaps greater agitation, Steele shrugged and drawled instead, 'One glass of wine, *for old times' sake,*' heavily stressed, 'is hardly likely to tempt anyone from the straight and narrow.'

'It's a beginning,' Matthew insisted righteously, then scowled with hard-eyed suspicion. 'What do you mean, "for old times' sake"?'

'Just that your fiancée and I are—er—friends, from way back,' Steele relayed for his doubtful benefit on what could only have been described as an expressively evocative note.

'Oh?' Matthew glared at Ravelle darkly—as if she hadn't been entitled to know any male apart from her assumed husband before she met him—then returned his gaze to his informant. 'And just how far back would that be?' he demanded curtly.

'About four years,' Steele was nothing loath to further his knowledge. 'Ravelle and I came to know each other rather well when we travelled on the same ship together. Or hasn't she told you about her trip to Japan yet?'

'Yes, I've told him . . . about everything I considered *worth* mentioning,' Ravelle sniped caustically, gaining her feet, and had the pleasure of knowing from the savage light which leapt into his eyes that her shaft had found its mark. She didn't know why he should now be going to such lengths to arouse Matthew's suspicions by alluding, however faintly, to their affair, but she certainly didn't plan to sit idly by and let him get away with it. She smiled chaffingly, perfunctorily. 'Now, if you'll all excuse me, I'll see if I can't give a hand with the coffee.'

CHAPTER THREE

THE room was more of a kitchenette than a full sized kitchen where Ravelle found Erin, but after her initial half frown of surprise that the area should have been so small when compared to the spacious sitting room, she surmised that it probably wasn't necessary for them to have anything larger since, if lunch had been an indication of their habits, they no doubt joined the resort guests for most of their meals.

Erin was busily arranging cups on a tray when Ravelle entered and offered diffidently, 'I was wondering if I could be of any help.'

'That's very kind of you, although there isn't really much to do except wait for the percolator,' the red-headed woman smiled back. 'I wouldn't say no to some company while I waited, though.' She inclined her head towards the other room, her lips curving wryly. 'How's it going inside?'

'Like skating on thin ice,' Ravelle grimaced ruefully. 'And I'm sorry Matthew's causing such a furore over something so trivial. I feel very guilty about you and your husband accepting the blame when if I'd left as I intended instead of talking to Steele,' even though he hadn't really given her a choice in the matter, 'then none of this would have happened.'

'Oh, don't let it worry you,' Erin discounted easily. 'When you deal with as many members of the public as we do, it's inevitable that you're not going to please everyone all the time. So,' she hunched her shoulders fatalistically, 'rather than have a disgruntled guest we usually prefer to bend with the breeze, as it were. It keeps the visitors happy and it's less wearing on us. Besides, your fiancé does, it seems, have at least some basis for his complaint. A lot of them don't even have that, believe me! Fortunately, though, they're in a minority. On the whole, we find most people are just looking to relax and enjoy their holidays without getting into any hassles.'

'Until a short time ago I was under the impression that that's what we intended too,' sighed Ravelle.

'Yes, well, that's the way of it sometimes, I guess,'

Erin laughed as she added a bowl of sugar to the tray. 'Although I must admit I was surprised at Steele stepping in as he did. That's most unlike him, and especially on such short acquaintance.' Two creases made their appearance between her brows and her glance turned quizzical. 'Or would I be right in assuming this *isn't* the first time you and he have met?'

Ravelle dropped her gaze discomfitedly to the top of the table. 'Yes, well, as a matter of fact, we did meet once, some years back,' she owned huskily, awkwardly. 'Not that that explains his attitude towards Matthew, though, because at the time we didn't exactly part on the—er—best of terms.'

'Oh?' Erin's reddish-brown brows flew to their highest peak now. 'I didn't think my personable brother-in-law had ever been on anything *but* the best of terms with any member of the opposite sex. Unless—unless . . .,' she faltered to a stop, her lips forming a circle of amazement as a thought came to her. 'You didn't by any chance meet him on a ship coming back from Japan, did you?'

As Steele had only just seen fit to inform Matthew and Vance of the venue for their meeting there was no point in keeping it a secret from Erin, so she gave her affirmation with a minimal, 'Yes.' Then couldn't refrain from immediately following it with a querying, 'But how did you guess that?'

'A shot in the dark,' the other woman revealed with a laugh. 'When Steele returned from that trip he was in the foulest mood I've ever seen him in, and he was almost impossible to talk to for weeks—no, months—afterwards. So, when you said the pair of you hadn't had a particularly amicable parting, I put two and two together. . .'

'And unfortunately got five,' Ravelle finished decisively for her.

'You mean, you weren't the reason for his black mood?' Erin sounded disappointed.

'That's exactly what I mean!' was the emphatic answer, but with an uncontrollable tinge of bitterness to it. How could she have been? She had refused to accept his contemptible pay-off money, and that would surely have put him in a pleased mood, not a displeased one! Unless of course, her thoughts ran on, he had taken exception to that refusal because it denied him the salve to his conscience that the offer had obviously been meant to be? Even so, it was still hardly likely to have put him out of sorts for the length of time Erin had implied, she reasoned with herself. No, there had to be some other cause.

'In any case,' she continued aloud, 'didn't he have a fiancée at the time? I understood he did have. Or was he in the habit of forgetting that trifling detail?'

'Hey, look, I wasn't meaning to suggest there was anything going on between the pair of you,' Erin hurried to assure her. 'I just thought you might have been able to provide us—well, me anyway,' she amended with a wryly honest grin, 'with some clue as to what did upset him to such an extent. It was so unlike him!' Suddenly her forehead furrowed and she eyed Ravelle with a half probing, half humorous look. 'That's the second time I've said that about Steele in almost as many minutes, and for each occasion you've been somewhere in the picture. Are you absolutely positive you don't know what caused that grim state of his four years back?'

'I'm positive,' Ravelle replied with feigned impassivity. 'Perhaps he had an argument with his fiancée.

'Well, I don't know about with Kathleen, but he certainly had one hell of a set-to with his father when he called the engagement off, I can tell you! His father swore he'd disown him, and lord only knows what else he didn't threaten him with in order to try to have the marriage take place, but he might as well have saved himself the energy and he really should have known better than to try such tactics. You can *ask* Steele to do something, but it's a fatal mistake to attempt to *force* him into doing it, because you'll find yourself up against a brick wall every time.'

'Although his father presumably relented in the end, since from what Steele said earlier I gather he's still a director of their family company.'

'Hah, like blazes he relented! That man didn't know the meaning of the word. In fact, it never ceases to amaze me—but I'm eternally grateful for it—that none of his five children take after him. They're more like their grandfather, a tremendous old chap who lives out at Longreach, and who was quite instrumental, so I hear, in diversifying their interests into real estate, etcetera, instead of just sheep and cattle. No, it certainly wasn't because his father forgave him that Steele's still a director in the company,' Erin asserted vigorously, returning to her original line of thought. 'That only came about owing to two things over which he had no control —the first being the rest of the family refusing point-blank to sanction his plans, which made it somewhat more difficult for him to carry them out, while the second was a light plane crash which he didn't survive.

'He's dead?' Ravelle gasped, trying to assimilate the unexpected information. She hadn't liked the man but, even so she could only feel shock at the idea of his having died so suddenly. 'Maybe he was psychic,' she went on in a musing voice. 'He never did like flying, did he?'

Briefly, Erin stared at her curiously, and then she began to smile. 'For a while there I thought you must have been too. But I guess you would have met him, as well as Steele, on that trip, wouldn't you?'

'Mmm.'

Green eyes twinkled with understanding. 'You ran foul of his cutting tongue too, did you, Ravelle?' She tilted her head to one side disarmingly. 'You don't mind

me calling you by your first name, do you? You're
welcome to use mine, you know.'

'Thank you, and no, I don't mind at all,' Ravelle
smiled. 'As for . . .'

'Come on, Erin, what's keeping the coffee?' interrupted Steele's slightly rough-edged voice from the
doorway.

'Nothing, it's just about ready.' His sister-in-law un-
plugged the percolator and poured the steaming coffee
into a jug which she then placed on the tray. 'Why,
what's the rush?'

'In order to retain at least some of the resort in our
hands,' he quipped sarcastically. Turning to Ravelle,
he elucidated in the same stinging tone, 'Your fiancé sure
believes in making the most of his opportunities, doesn't
he? He's already hit Vance for two free fishing trips, and
a *guided* tour of Hermitage. Now he's angling for some
riding lessons as well!' He made a contemptuous sound
deep in his throat. 'I knew right from the start that I
wasn't going to like that puffed-up little toad, and so far
all he's done is confirm my judgment.'

Appalled though she was by Matthew's apparent
exploitation of the circumstances, Ravelle just couldn't
let that go unchallenged, and her chin lifted aggres-
sively. 'Then, at a guess, I'd say that makes you even,
because I've no doubt he's not exactly impressed by your
overbearing and arbitrary behaviour either, Steele
Cunningham!' she flared hotly, whirling past him, and
making for the sitting room.

'Well, we know who won that encounter, don't we?'
Matthew rubbed his hands together in undisguised satisfaction as he and Ravelle left their hosts' quarters some
long, embarrassing—for Ravelle, at least—minutes
later, after he had finally succeeded in extracting as much
goodwill as he was able to from Vance. 'That'll teach

that damned high-handed friend of yours not to inter-
fere with us in future.'

'He's no friend of mine!' she contradicted sharply.
Anything but, in fact. 'Although I hardly think what
happened in there is likely to have any effect on Steele.
After all, it was his brother who was trying to meet you
halfway, certainly not him!' That was, until even the
easy-going Vance had decided enough was enough and
began to show all too clearly that his hospitality wasn't
by any means inexhaustible—something, to her morti-
fication, Matthew hadn't appeared to realise. 'In any
case, I shouldn't let your success go to your head, if I
were you. They were doing quite a creditable snow job on
you too while they were at it, you know. The advantages
gained weren't altogether one-sided, and I'm sure that if
it hadn't suited their purposes you wouldn't have
received as many concessions as you did.'

'You think I could have asked for more?'

'Would that have been possible?' she couldn't help
countering drily. At one stage she had been fully expecting him to suggest they have their whole holiday for free.

'My word, it was possible,' he retorted. 'And why
shouldn't I? They can afford it. They must have a mint
to own one of these places, and what they gave us is
peanuts compared to what they must make from these
islands.'

'That isn't the point, though, is it? Quite frankly, I
don't think we were entitled to anything, and that
applies whether they can afford it or not.'

'What, and meekly crawl away after that half-dressed
lout had threatened me?'

'Oh, Matthew!' She shook her head helplessly. 'If you
hadn't lost your cool over me drinking a little wine, he
probably wouldn't have said anything to you at all.'

'Whether I lost my cool or not had nothing to do with
it! He had no right to poke his nose in where it didn't

belong!' he gritted furiously. 'Sitting there like some
itinerant beachcomber! It shouldn't have been allowed!'

'Well, it is a beach resort, Matthew,' she emphasised
gently, persuasively. 'Nor was it as if the restaurant was
packed at the time. Apart from that couple down the far
end, we were the only ones there.'

His blue eyes swept over her resentfully. 'So you're
taking his side, are you?'

'Not likely!' she scoffed. 'If you must know, I didn't
even expect to be talking to him when I saw he was also
staying here. The last time I had any contact with him
was enough for me, thanks!'

Matthew looked as if he wasn't certain whether he
should believe her or not. 'Yet you deliberately sat
drinking with him while I was waiting for you,' he half
accused, half puzzled.

As they came out from beneath the trees the beach
lay before them, but on this occasion Ravelle stared at
the inviting panorama unseeingly, a somewhat bitter
laugh issuing from her slender throat.

'Not from choice, I can assure you,' she relayed heavily.
'He just wouldn't take no for an answer.'

'Then why defend his subsequent actions so adamantly?'

With a sigh she looked away from him and out to sea.
How could she tell him it wasn't so much Steele's actions
that she was defending as it was his own she was condemning? Of the two, she was sorry to have to admit
that she considered Matthew's behaviour to have been
the least becoming, but she very much doubted he would
appreciate her saying as much.

Shrugging, she avoided giving a direct response. 'I
wasn't aware that I was, and it definitely wasn't my
intention,' she offered quietly. 'But do we have to talk
about him any more? As far as I'm concerned, he's just
one of many staying here, and if I don't speak to him

again during the remainder of our visit it won't be worrying me.'

He looked at her closely. 'Do you really mean that?'

'Of course I do!' she exclaimed, eyes widening in surprise. Then, with a comprehending smile curving her soft mouth, 'There was no need for you to have warned Steele away from me, Matthew. I could spend the whole day in his company without once even looking like falling for that brand of vibrant maleness he exudes so effortlessly.' Having been a victim of it once, there was no likelihood of it happening again! 'Beauty *is* only skin deep, and it's the steadfastness underneath that counts, not the attractive packaging. You've stood by Sam and me for a long time now. I'm not about to desert you for the first handsome face that comes along.' And especially not when it belonged to one Steele Cunningham!

For the first time since leaving the mainland that morning Matthew suddenly seemed to relax, the ruefully apologetic smile he sent her relieving the tenseness of his expression.

'I'm sorry, Ravelle, I guess I shouldn't have needed that explained to me. I know you've never even looked at another man since we've been going together.' He hunched one shoulder selfconsciously. 'Knowing I couldn't compete, I suppose deep down I've been nervous of any brawny, suntanned specimens we might encounter here, and then when I found you cosily chatting with someone who was the embodiment of all my worst fears . . . well, I'm afraid I rather let those apprehensions get the better of me. Not that I regret the concessions I obtained from the Cunninghams, mind you,' he put in swiftly, incisively. 'As I said, it was only a drop in the ocean to them and in my opinion fully deserved, but I do feel a sense of remorse for having temporarily misplaced my faith in you. I'm well aware you're not of a promiscuous disposition—you never have been—and it was wrong of me to suspect that you may have been changing now.'

Ravelle acknowledged the last of his apology uncomfortably, her insides churning with guilt. Why, oh, why hadn't she told him the truth about her daughter? After that touching avowal of his faith in her morals, and now that he had actually met—and disliked on sight—Samara's father, there was no way in the world she could ever tell him now! And if he should, by any chance, find out by accident. . . . Oh, God, that didn't bear thinking about! No, the only thing she could do was to continue in the lie her parents had woven and which she had accepted, unwitting of the consequences.

'Anyway, I'm not sure I know what you mean by saying you can't compete,' she decided to bypass his last remarks in favour of a previous one. 'Just because you're not as tall,' he was only five centimetres or so taller than her one hundred and sixty-five, 'or as heavily built as someone who's a hundred and eighty-eight centimetres and has muscles to spare,' she unknowingly approximated Steele's measurements as a comparison, 'that doesn't by any means make you any less of a person. As for the other—well,' she turned her face up to the sun with a grin, 'a tan is easy to come by here.'

'For those with a naturally warm tint to their skin like you, maybe,' he grimaced.

'For you too if you take it in easy stages.' Her eyes smiled encouragement. 'Ten or fifteen minutes a day for the first week, and it won't be long before you're as brown as everyone else.'

'Since I can't recall ever having been any colour except white, or vivid agonising red, I think I'll just take your word for it and remain covered up, all the same,' he said, refusing to be swayed.

'You won't even come out on the reef with me, just once?' she cajoled.

'No way!' His rejection came with unswerving resolution. 'With all that bending over to see the coral, or whatever, I know exactly where the sun will catch me—right on the back of the legs—and having been sunburnt behind the knees once before, I can assure you I'm not about to invite another dose of the same.'

Disappointed that she hadn't been able to persuade him into accompanying her, Ravelle sighed and let the matter drop. He had apparently convinced himself he was going to get burnt and it was just as obvious nothing she said to the contrary was going to make him change his mind.

'Well, what shall we do for the rest of the afternoon, then?' she asked.

'Play table tennis, naturally!' Matthew seemed astonished she should even have to enquire. 'That is what we planned, isn't it?'

'I'd forgotten.' Or hoped he had? she wondered to herself wryly as they turned for the main buildings.

'Of course we may have some trouble getting a table now,' he complained with a return to his peevish tone.

'I shouldn't think so,' she shrugged. Who else but Matthew would want to be inside on a day like this? 'By the look of things just about everyone is either swimming or waiting for the tide to drop a little more before going out on the reef.'

'Meaning, that's what you would prefer to be doing?'

'Not really,' she lied in order to keep the peace. 'There'll be other days.'

'Mmm, you can see it when Vance takes me on one of those fishing trips he promised me,' Matthew allowed magnanimously.

'Thanks!' Ravelle was unable to stop retorting drily, her brown eyes widening. 'Those concessions you won,' or should that have been wrung? 'from him are exclusively for yourself, are they?'

'Oh, no, you're included in the tour of Hermitage and the riding lessons, but I don't really consider fishing to be a woman's game. You know how averse you are to removing the hook from anything you happen to catch.' His reminder was patronisingly made.

She still wouldn't have minded going along, even if only for the experience, but that he apparently hadn't considered. 'You're not averse to going out in a boat now, I gather,' she deduced in ironic tones.

Matthew at least had the grace to look a little discomfited. 'No, well—er—after thinking over what you had to say about it earlier, I decided it was too good an opportunity to miss when the chance was there to get a couple of trips without cost.'

'I see.' Her golden blonde hair swept across a bare shoulder as she tilted her head speculatively to one side. 'Would you have gone if you'd had to pay for them?'

'Possibly not,' he replied shortly, then continued in a hardening tone, 'Although what that has to do with anything, I don't know. If something's to be had for free, why should I pay for it?'

'Why, indeed!' Her mouth shaped wryly. 'However, I wasn't attempting to make you feel guilty, Matthew, I was only enquiring out of interest's sake.'

'Perhaps that's just as well, then, because I certainly don't feel guilty in the slightest,' he denied promptly, haughtily. Entering the main building, he added in peremptory tones, 'So now I suggest we drop the subject, hmm?'

'If you like,' she acquiesced dispassionately, since the atmosphere between them did seem to be cooling by the minute and she wasn't anxious for it to deteriorate any further.

Once inside the games room—deserted, as she had anticipated—and they began playing, Matthew immediately began to recover his good spirits. The more

so when he beat her by a wide margin each time. Nevertheless, after six such easy conquests even he found the
game starting to pall, and when she retrieved the ball
after his last winning smash, preparing to start serving
again, he laid down his bat on the table and expelled an
impatient breath.

'I know you weren't really in favour of playing,
Ravelle, but surely, even if only as a favour to me, you
could put a little more effort into it, couldn't you?' he
demanded.

'I was putting in as much as I could,' she returned indignantly. 'It's not my fault if you're the better player. I
don't usually beat you, anyway, so why get all uptight
about it now?'

'Because I know you can play better, that's why!
Maybe if you concentrated you'd find it would help!'

'I am concentrating!' she flared. 'I can't help it if my
game's a little off today.' ·

With his back to the doorway Matthew couldn't see
there was another couple entering the room, but
Ravelle could, and her face flamed in embarrassment
that Steele and his companion—the other redhead with
whom he had shared lunch—should be the ones to hear
her fiancé snap back sarcastically,

'Well, you're the only one who can improve it, so try
a little harder, why don't you?'

As he strolled past their table with easy grace, his chest
now covered by a dark green T-shirt, a mocking smile
began playing about Steele's lips. 'Good lord, are you
in trouble again, Ravelle? You really can't be doing the
right thing by the man,' he taunted, but didn't slow his
stride to a halt.

The girl beside him smiled archly, her expression
saying all too plainly that she never experienced any
such difficulty, and Ravelle gritted her teeth furiously.
How dared he, after all he'd done, hold *her* up to ridicule

in front of his . . . wife? . . . fiancée . . . girl-friend? If anyone should feel humiliated by their meeting, it should be him, not her!

From the other end of the table came Matthew's voice in expectedly, maddeningly approving tones. 'For once he's said something with which I wholeheartedly agree. Your attitude has been rather a selfish one since we arrived, Ravelle. You expect me to fall in with whatever you want to do, and yet the first time I suggest something you can't even be bothered to display the smallest amount of interest.'

She was being selfish! Ravelle seethed resentfully. So far he'd dismissed every solitary suggestion she had made! But, conscious as she was of the pair searching through a wall cupboard behind her, she held her tongue and kept her comments to herself. She wasn't going to air her grievances for Steele's undoubted amusement.

'I'm sorry,' she murmured quietly, grudgingly, in lieu. 'Do you want to play another game?'

'That depends, doesn't it?' And when she frowned her puzzlement, Matthew enlightened caustically, 'On whether you're intended to exert yourself or not.'

A deep-toned laugh sounded from Steele, involuntarily conjuring up remembered pleasures from another time, another place, and causing her breathing to at first slow and then race unsteadily as she fought against their subtle appeal. For the moment Matthew was completely forgotten. She couldn't concentrate on him and bring her unruly senses to heel at the same time, and quelling those painfully disruptive images was of paramount importance for her peace of mind.

Not surprisingly, Matthew saw her sudden preoccupation as having a different cause altogether, and in order to reclaim her attention he rapped determinedly on the table with his bat.

'If that's any indication of your interest, I can see I'm wasting my time,' he bit out exasperatedly.

'What?' Ravelle shook her head bewilderedly, and attempting to focus outwardly now instead of inwardly. 'Oh, yes—I'm sorry,' she apologised distractedly. 'I—I'll certainly do my best. Do you want to serve, or shall I?'

'You may as well, since you've got the ball, I suppose,' he heaved.

Much to her relief this time she did manage to do better, but unhappily only until Steele and his companion —having presumably located whatever they had been looking for—drew abreast of the table as they were leaving the room and then, to Ravelle's dismay, stopped to watch.

From that moment on her play went from bad to worse, and when Steele drawled mock-sympathetically, 'Sorry, did we make you nervous?' after Matthew had finally come out the winner by an even wider margin than previously, she started to wonder if that hadn't been the effect he planned to have all along.

'You must have done, because she was doing quite well until you arrived,' put in Matthew in an unaccountably understanding voice.

The redheaded girl pouted prettily. 'Oh, dear, and we only stopped so that Steele could introduce me, seeing we'll all be having dinner together this evening. I'm Chantal Gregory, Erin's sister,' she disclosed with a smile.

Matthew approached quickly from his end of the table. 'Matthew Inglis,' he replied. 'And this is my fiancée, Ravelle Fenton.'

'How do you do?' Ravelle returned the other girl's smile, her brain swiftly sifting the information it had just received. Well, this curvaceous young woman with the milky white skin and pale green eyes obviously wasn't Steele's wife, or a new fiancée. So what did that leave . . .

girl-friend? Or just one of the family? Annoyed with herself for even bothering to analyse their relationship, she lifted her head high, and found herself watching a frown descend on to Steele's forehead.

'Fenton?' he repeated in a questioning tone. 'I thought you said you'd been married?'

'I—I have,' Ravelle confirmed nervously. 'I just decided to—to keep my own name and adopt the prefix Ms, that's all.'

'Didn't your husband mind?' queried Chantal, wide-eyed.

'No, he was—er—very understanding.'

Beneath sardonically lifting brows gunmetal grey eyes fixed her with a goading glance. 'Don't you intend to become *Mrs* Inglish either?' Steele quizzed.

Ravelle shrugged selfconsciously, moving restlessly under that too astute gaze. 'I really hadn't thought about . . .'

'Of course she will!' Matthew broke in firmly. 'No wife of mine will ever have any other name but Inglis.'

Steele didn't comment, but merely flicked her an expectant look—as if to tell her the ball was now back in her court—which had her swallowing convulsively and stammering, 'If th-that's what Matthew w-wants, then n-naturally I will.'

'That was a rapid turn-around, wasn't it?' he mocked.

'I don't know what you mean,' she murmured, eyeing him warily.

'Well, you gave in so quickly on this occasion that one wonders why you made such a point of it previously.'

'The circumstances were different,' she all but whispered shakily, wishing he would just leave. If he asked enough questions there was always the chance either he, or Matthew, could become suspicious of her answers. 'And if you don't mind, I—I'd rather not talk about my first marriage. I find it very upsetting,' she added for her own defence

'Oh, I'm sure you must,' Steele granted, but with such a cynical inflection in his voice that she shivered apprehensively. Linking his arm with Chantal's, he looked to Matthew enquiringly, 'We'll see you at dinner, then, shall we?'

'You will,' Matthew nodded positively.

Beside him, Ravelle watched the other two depart with her teeth worrying at her bottom lip. Even dining in the seclusion of Matthew's unit seemed preferable now that she knew Steele would also be joining them for the evening meal. It wasn't a contingency she had foreseen, and definitely wasn't one for which she was prepared!

CHAPTER FOUR

AFTER a refreshing shower, Ravelle applied very little in the way of make-up for the evening ahead. A touch of frosted shadow for her eyelids, a brushing of mascara for her already thick and curling lashes, and a coating of coral gloss to her softly curving lips. Her loosely waving blonde hair she pinned firmly into the french pleat that Matthew liked so much, and then slid the tiny gold drop earrings her parents had bought her for her last birthday through her ears. The dress she had chosen to wear was of a becoming apricot and apple green patterned acrylic which hugged her neat waist and draped gently over one shoulder, while her feet she slipped into a dainty pair of ankle-strapped sandals of matching green.

A glance at the slim watch encircling her wrist showed there was still some time before Matthew's arranged arrival and, lighting a cigarette, she wandered out on to the small private porch of her unit. Availing herself of

the front rail for a seat, she leant back against a roof
support and gazed apprehensively towards the community buildings which were now ablaze with lights, their
golden beams only serving to emphasise the velvet-dark
backdrop of the tropical night. She was, quite frankly, on
tenterhooks just at the thought of dining with Steele, and
in dread of what he might inadvertently—or even
deliberately, if his attitude of the afternoon was to be any
guide—reveal to Matthew. Why he should have
decided to walk so casually back into her life instead of
ignoring her, as she had planned to do to him, she had no
idea, but for the hundredth time since he'd done so
she found herself wishing he hadn't. He was all too easily
reviving memories she wanted to forget, and the knowledge that he could destroy her relationship with Matthew
with one careless word was just as disastrously playing
havoc with her nerves.

At the far end of the pool quite a number of guests
were beginning to gather for aperitifs, and the sound of
their happy voices as they discussed and laughed over
their various activities of the day had Ravelle sighing
wistfully. That was how she had imagined it would be
for Matthew and herself at the end of each day—relaxed
and carefree, not experiencing a churning, threatening
sense of impending disaster which would coil her insides
tighter than a spring.

After a while the crowd started to diminish as couples
and family groups made their way across to the cloth-
covered tables on the patio, a few heading inside the
restaurant itself, and surmising that Matthew would be
along at any minute, Ravelle returned to her room to
put out her cigarette then resumed her seat on the rail.
When he still hadn't put in an appearance some ten
minutes later a frown lowered on to her forehead as she
wondered what could possibly have been detaining him,
since it was almost unheard of for him to be late for an

appointment, and she decided to set off for his unit to find out.

She was almost to his door before she came across him, he was ambling down the steps to the path as if he had all the time in the world to spare, and she waited for him to join her with a perplexed look of her face.

'Your watch can't be keeping the correct time,' she deduced anxiously. 'We're almost a quarter of an hour late, you know.'

His acknowledging smile was more of a smirk. 'Yes, we are, aren't we?'

The creases in Ravelle's forehead became even deeper. 'You mean, you want to be late?' she questioned incredulously.

'Of course,' he returned in his most complacent manner. 'Otherwise I wouldn't be.'

'But—but why?' It didn't make sense to her.

'Why not?' he countered, shrugging. 'At least it's one way of showing them we don't intend kowtowing to their every command.'

That it was also rude and petty Ravelle didn't point out, judging it to be a waste of time at the moment. Instead, she exclaimed with some exasperation, 'For goodness' sake, Matthew, it was an invitation, not a command, and if you're that keen to flaunt your independence, why agree to have dinner with them at all?'

'Because I was entitled to it, naturally!'

Ravelle felt she could have disputed that statement too, but once again she let the matter ride. The last thing she wanted was an argument with her fiancé before facing the Cunninghams. She suspected it was going to be quite trying enough without that!

'I thought you were feeling a little more kindly disposed towards them from your manner when Steele spoke to us in the games room,' she mused speculatively, rather than pursue his previous comment.

'Yes, well, I did find him somewhat less abrasive on that occasion,' he allowed reluctantly. 'Although that was purely incidental, you understand. I don't want them thinking that just because they deign to speak to us, I'm going to forget what happened previously.'

'Oh, no, of course not,' she endorsed, drily tongue-in-cheek. How could they possibly when he clearly meant to remind them at every opportunity?

'I'm glad you agree with me.' Matthew nodded his satisfaction, taking her words literally. 'It's always best to present a united front to people like these, then they know you mean business.'

He made it sound as if they were at war, but as his sentiments so very nearly echoed hers—if for differing reasons—Ravelle was only too willing to concur with his proposal and, linking her arm through his, she walked into the restaurant with her head angled defiantly high.

Their hosts were sitting at a large round table close to the open glass doors. As near to being outside as possible without actually being there, Ravelle noted wryly as they made their way across the room. Steele and his brother, similarly dressed in faultless custom-made pants and silk knit shirts, rose upright at their approach and as Vance held out one of the two vacant chairs between his own and Chantal's for her, Ravelle acknowledged his action with a quick smile.

'Thank you, and I'm sorry we're late,' she apologised, taking the seat offered.

'That's all right,' asserted Erin, her friendly expression encompassing Matthew too as the men seated themselves. 'You're here now, and we've been too busy talking to do more than order something to drink in any case.'

'While we're on that subject . . .' broke in Vance, turning to their guests enquiringly, 'what would you care for in that regard? Fruit juice, some soft drinks, or we also have some non-alcoholic wines if you would prefer?'

Matthew shook his head peremptorily, indicating the stainless steel pitcher in the centre of the table, much as he had done to the waitress at lunchtime. 'There's no substitute for water, we'll stick to that, thanks.'

'Ravelle?' Vance still sought her choice, even though her fiancé had implied he had decided for both of them.

'No, the water will do fine, thank you,' she smiled selfconsciously. Actually, she wouldn't have minded at least trying the non-alcoholic wine, but Matthew would no doubt consider that a direct flouting of his wishes and react accordingly, and that she didn't want at any cost.

From almost directly opposite Steele's sardonic grey eyes met hers challengingly as he produced a packet of cigarettes and, flipping back the top, held it out towards her. 'But you do still smoke, I presume?' he enquired tauntingly.

Ravelle refused his offer with a hasty shake of her head. 'Only very rarely,' she replied tautly, but determined not to let that shrewdly knowing gaze disconcert her. It was still a bone of contention between Matthew and herself that she hadn't given up the habit altogether, in accordance with his constant urgings.

'And never when she's with me,' put in Matthew sharply.

'Oh, I see.' Steele's lips quirked provokingly. 'Then of course I apologise for having tempted Ravelle to transgress once again. I wouldn't want to see more dissension between you two today.'

For that snide effort Ravelle sent him a fulminating glare from smouldering brown eyes, but Matthew, thinking he had won a victory in view of Steele's supposed apology, accepted the speciously worded regrets with self-satisfaction.

'Mmm, well, I suppose you weren't to know,' he allowed generously. 'I expect Ravelle's changed in many ways since you knew her.'

'So it would appear,' Steele conceded on a dry note, his glance taunting as it rested on the girl opposite. 'You must exert quite a considerable influence.'

Matthew's expression immediately changed to one of smug complacency, causing Ravelle's resentment to soar. How dared they discuss her as if she wasn't present! And as for her fiancé . . . Couldn't he see that Steele was only amusing himself at their expense? Or was he too occupied lapping up what he believed were words of praise to care? she fumed.

Fortunately, Erin was either more perceptive, or at least sensed how Ravelle was feeling, because she promptly took the opportunity to insert, 'I'm so sorry, I don't think you've met my sister Chantal yet, have you?'

'As a matter of fact I introduced myself while they were playing table tennis this afternoon, although I'm afraid that by stopping to watch, Steele and I seemed to put Ravelle completely off her game,' Chantal relayed with an irritating laugh. She slanted Ravelle an amused, sidelong glance. 'Did you improve once we'd left?'

'Not to a great extent,' was the wry admission.

The redheaded girl turned her attention to Matthew. 'Then perhaps you might care to give me a game next time instead,' she suggested archly. 'I'm quite proficient at most indoor games, aren't I, Steele?'

'That you are,' his confirmation was lazily drawled, but accompanied by such an evocative expression that Ravelle found herself wondering—with unfamiliar acerbity—just which particular indoor activity he was meaning.

Matthew, meanwhile, was only too willing to accept the offer. 'Yes, I think I'd like that,' he smiled pleasurably. 'Being fair-skinned . . . like yourself,' appreciatively, 'I do usually prefer indoor pastimes myself. When would you suggest we have our match?'

'Well, I wouldn't make it for tomorrow, if I were you,' interposed Vance. 'That is, not unless you've changed your mind about going fishing.'

'No! No, of course I haven't,' Matthew went to great pains to assure him, and obviously fearful of forfeiting any of his prized concessions. 'Why, have you arranged something?'

'A trip to Tern Cay,' he was advised. 'It's an all-day venture, and normally very worthwhile. There'll be about a dozen of us going altogether.'

'Oh, that many.' Matthew sounded disappointed that he wasn't to be the only passenger.

'You'd rather wait for a day when there might be less?'

It was almost possible to see the wheels of Matthew's brain ticking over as he weighed up the likelihood of his missing out entirely if such an eventuality failed to occur.

'No, I'll come,' he made his decision swiftly. 'What time do we leave?'

'As soon as possible after an early breakfast.'

'I'm not expected to provide anything, am I?' Matthew queried suspiciously, and making Ravelle wince at his avaricious attitude.

'Not in the way of food or fishing equipment, if that's what you mean. The resort supplies all those,' Vance disclosed levelly, if a little curtly. 'Anything of a more personal nature, though, is up to you, of course.'

'And talking of food . . .' again it was Erin who judged a change in topic could be beneficial, 'here comes Beverley to take our order, and Ravelle and Matthew haven't even seen the menu yet,' she said as one of the sarong-clad waitresses approached the table with pad and pencil in hand.

Provided with a copy of the sky blue and gold printed bill of fare, Ravelle chose quickly and somewhat meagrely, not wanting to take advantage of their hosts' hospitality. On the other hand, Matthew displayed no such reticence and made his selection with a liberality that had her flushing uncomfortably at the amount, and the length of time it took the waitress to note it all down. Even so, amidst her embarrassment, she still found time to hope, for her fiancé's sake, that he didn't have cause to regret his extravagance on the morrow once he was out to sea, otherwise some might consider it nothing more than poetic justice.

'Perhaps we could have our game the day after tomorrow, then?' Chantal returned to their original subject as soon as Beverley had departed with their orders.

'Why not tomorrow night?' countered Matthew enthusiastically.

If his fishing trip affected him as much as the journey from the mainland had, Ravelle very much doubted he would be in any condition to play tomorrow night, but apparently he was choosing to overlook that slight consideration, she noted wryly.

In any case, Chantal was to veto the idea herself. 'Uh-uh! Not at night, that's when we have our discos,' she explained, indicating the quartet on the patio who were playing background music at the moment. 'And I love dancing . . . don't you?'

He hunched one shoulder indifferently, his eagerness decidedly waning. 'It's all right, I suppose, provided it's not too frenetic.'

'Then, just for you, we'll have to see they play a greater amount of slower numbers, won't we?' Chantal smiled coyly.

Believing he had scored another success, Matthew promptly became more cheerful, but Ravelle couldn't make up her mind whether the other girl was serious or not. And if she was, then it was equally difficult to fathom just why she should have been going to such lengths to

insinuate herself into Matthew's good graces. It wasn't
as if her fiancé had the type of looks which immediately
turned female heads—they were fairly formed, but
certainly nothing outstanding—and as the girl on his
other side wasn't exactly short in that department herself,
nor of money, judging by the cream-coloured silk dress
she was wearing, then it was probably reasonable to
suppose she could have had her pick of just about any
male on the island. So why was she so intent on indulging
Matthew when he was not only engaged, but had also
shown himself to be somewhat less than good company
ever since his arrival?

The idea that she might have been doing it in order to
ensure he stayed off the Cunningham's backs as much as
possible presented itself briefly but was rapidly discarded.
Since Vance's good nature had been strained to the
utmost by Matthew's demands during the afternoon,
Ravelle thought it highly unlikely he would be prepared
to meet her fiancé halfway again, no matter what the
reason. Eventually, the only solution which appeared to
make any sense was that Chantal was just one of those
women who liked every male within sight—no matter
who—to feel the force of their charm and was merely
seeking to add another admirer to her collection.

In one regard, the thought that Chantal's interest had
been occasioned by just such a desire afforded Ravelle no
great qualms on her own behalf, at least not where
Matthew was concerned. Past knowledge more than
amply reassured her that he wasn't the type to indulge in
a faithless flirtation, even though he might have been
basking uninhibitedly in the light of the other girl's
attention. What did cause her some anxiety, however,
was the fact that as the meal progressed with unnerving
slowness owing to the number of courses Matthew had
seen fit to select, his preoccupation with whatever Erin's
sister had to impart tended to leave Ravelle to parry

Steele's mockingly punctuated remarks on her own.

An extremely perturbing exercise in view of the subtle swing in his attitude to a seemingly less hostile one in Matthew's favour, but an increasingly harsh one for her. The cause of the change she couldn't even begin to ascertain, and especially not when every faculty she possessed was concentrated on a single plan of action—to escape his potentially dangerous presence as soon as possible. One word from him about their last night on board ship and . . .! She shuddered inwardly at the thought of what Matthew's reaction might be.

'So when are you and Matthew getting married?' It was Steele again, at his drawling, probing, best.

'We haven't—er—set a date as yet,' Ravelle told him jerkily. When nothing came from her fiancé she sent him a swift glance, only to find him listening to one of Chantal's asides, and with a self-conscious raising of one golden-skinned shoulder, went on tautly, 'We thought it best to wait until we'd saved enough for a deposit on a home of our own.'

'In these days of rising inflation, that's rather on a par with a dog attempting to catch its own tail, isn't it?'

The goading amusement in his voice was like salt being rubbed into Ravelle's already raw nerves, and her nails dug crescent moons into her palms as her hands clenched in her lap. 'More than likely!' she owned heatedly. 'But, unfortunately, not all of us can be born into feathered nests. Some of us have to make our own!'

'Then I would have thought you'd be well on your way to achieving that by now!' he retorted with such savage intensity that she could only stare at him in confused bewilderment.

'I d-don't know what you mean,' she stammered.

'Your first husband,' he enlightened her on a more moderate, but no less terse note. 'Surely you must have been the recipient of whatever assets he had. Plus a monetary remuneration in the form of insurance, compensation, social benefits, or something similar payable after his death.'

Strangely, Ravelle had the feeling that hadn't been what he was meaning at all, but as she couldn't think of any other possible reason for his comment, she had no choice but to accept the explanation offered.

'He—he didn't have any assets, or—or insurance,' she made up her answer as she went along. 'Nor could I claim any compensation because he wasn't covered. As for social benefits—well, I get child endowment for Samara, of course, but as I have a job I didn't really think it would be worthwhile applying for any other.'

'Samara?' he repeated attentively. 'Is that what you called your daughter?'

She nodded silently.

'Oh, dear, how tragic for you to have been widowed and left with a child as well at your age,' commiserated Erin, two furrows of sincere concern appearing between her brows. 'I quite imagined your coming marriage to Matthew would be your first, yet here you are a mother already. But how lucky you are to have a little girl. Vance and I have twin sons,' she confided with a smile at her husband, 'but we would have loved to have had a daughter too. Unfortunately, though, it doesn't appear thus far as if the Cunninghams are very keen on producing girls this generation.' She gave a rueful laugh. 'To date, Vance's mother has been presented with six grandchildren altogether, but without one granddaughter amongst them.' Leaning her elbows on the table, she rested her chin on linked fingers to enquire interestedly, 'How old is your little girl?'

'Three,' Ravelle half smiled uneasily.

'And a quarter.' Beside her Matthew suddenly returned to the general conversation at the worst possible time to amend with unaccustomed joviality. 'Sam's birthday is the twenty-eighth of May, remember, and she'd be most upset if you forgot those extra months.'

'Yes, well, I was only generalising,' she excused in strangled tones, and unable to control the rush of colour which flooded into her cheeks. Across the table Steele's smoky grey eyes were regarding her consideringly from beneath half lowered lids and she swung her gaze to Erin rapidly, desperate to find a safe subject. 'And your boys, how old are they?' she asked throatily.

'Nearly ten,' their mother smiled proudly. 'I expect you'll meet them some time while you're here, but in the evenings we do an early tea for the children so that parents can get them off to bed before they have their own dinners. Most people seem to prefer the arrangement —us amongst them—rather than keeping the smaller ones up until all hours, then at least they know they can take their time over their meal and enjoy the evening's entertainment with a clear conscience.'

'That sounds reasonable,' Ravelle nodded understandingly. 'And your sons live on the island with you all the time, do they? I bet they love that.'

'Mmm, too much so at times, I'm afraid,' Erin confessed with a rueful laugh. 'It makes correspondence lessons—with me deputising as teacher—seem very dreary when there's all that,' she waved a hand in the general direction of the beach and lagoon, 'waiting for them outside. I have to keep a very close eye on them when they're doing their schoolwork, otherwise they're off as soon as my back is turned. So if you ever see two young boys around—always together, and looking like two peas in a pod—before eleven in the morning, you can tell them from me to get themselves back inside if they know what's good for them,' she advised with another laugh.

Feeling her period of danger at having her secret exposed had been passed satisfactorily, Ravelle was able to laugh with her. 'After that, their time's their own, is it?'

'More or less, until later in the afternoon when they have to put in another couple of hours,' Erin grinned. 'When we first came here I tried keeping normal school times, but I soon found it just wasn't practical and that by midday their interest in what they were doing had disappeared completely. Now I start them at eight because it's cooler then and they're always up early anyway, then give them a long break in the middle of the day instead of trying to force them to concentrate for five or six hours straight.'

In surroundings such as existed at Morning Retreat, Ravelle could easily see how that might be a problem. 'They're also identical twins, are they?' she asked next in an effort to avoid a lull.

'Very definitely.' It was Vance who answered this time, wryly. 'Although as they've grown older certain slight differences have begun to manifest themselves . . . thank goodness.'

A humorous smile curved Ravelle's mouth upwards. 'In other words, it used to be impossible to tell them apart,' she guessed.

'For strangers, it still is, but not for us, I'm glad to say,' advised Erin with obvious relief. 'As Vance said, some differences are beginning to appear, and now of course because they're typically adventurous boys we have the incontrovertible proof of differing scars. Craig has one on his knee through falling on the coral, and Dion has one on the back of his left hand where he was bitten by a horse.'

'Not by one of those used for trail rides on Hermitage, I hope,' inserted Matthew reprovingly.

'Oh, no,' Vance hastened to disclaim, even as he exchanged a dry look with his brother at their guest's penchant for censure. 'This happened a few years ago while we were visiting my grandfather's property. No, I think you'll find all the mounts on Hermitage are docile enough. They're all expressly chosen for their temperament.'

'Well, that's something,' Matthew acknowledged grudgingly. 'As long as whoever does the choosing knows when they're about.'

Chantal gave a delighted chuckle. 'Oh, I think you can rest easy on that point, Matthew,' she counselled. 'Steele's been dealing with animals all his life and if he doesn't know a good horse from a bad one then no one does.'

'*You* select them?' Matthew aimed a lowering, not quite believing, glance across the table to the man opposite.

'Uh-huh,' drawled Steele laconically. 'Why, don't you think I'd be suitably qualified?'

'I wouldn't know,' conceded Matthew stiffly, wary now of jumping to conclusions a second time where this man was concerned, and especially in view of Chantal's comment. 'But living here, I wouldn't have thought . . .'

'Ah, but I don't normally live here,' Steele cut in smoothly. 'I'm only visiting for a couple of weeks in order to check the cattle breeding programme we've established on Hermitage. The resort was a proposition Vance suggested the family should try since Erin has considerable experience in the accommodation field, but first and foremost we're graziers.' His eyes moved slightly to cover the rather tense figure on his brother's right, his gaze narrowing. 'Or is that something *else* Ravelle has decided to keep you in the dark about?'

Just recovering from the realisation that Erin and her sister were members of *the* Gregory family that had hotels in every major town along the eastern seaboard—that casual 'accommodation field' had been the understatement of the year, she decided sardonically—Ravelle wasn't prepared for that last acrid addition, nor for what she suspected was its inherent double meaning, and momentarily she was frozen in an agony of suspense for fear of what Steele might insinuate next for her fiancé's edification.

'Goodness, Ravelle, you've gone as white as a sheet! Do you feel all right?'

It was Erin's anxious voice that broke in on her anguished thoughts, but it was Steele's unyielding expression her apprehensive gaze connected with before she began rubbing her fingers absently against her temples and turned away.

'I—I'm sorry, it must be the—the heat,' she fabricated with a faint apologetic smile. 'If you don't mind, I think—I think I'd like to get some fresh air.'

Rising to her feet, she found Matthew standing with her. 'I'll come with you,' he offered, unexpectedly solicitous. He normally had no time for others who were unwell.

'Is there anything I can get for you?' asked Vance, also on his feet now.

'No, really, please don't bother,' she dismissed his offer quickly. 'I'm sure I shall be okay once I'm outside.' And away from your intimidating brother, she added mutely, bitterly.

While they had been finishing their meal, most of the other diners had moved out on to the patio in order to dance to the more lively music the band was now playing and, skirting around them, Ravelle headed for a poolside table and chairs out of sight of their hosts.

For a few minutes she sat quietly, enjoying the cooling sea breeze which was caressing her heated skin, and gradually relaxing now that Steele wasn't around to keep her continually on edge. Then, unwittingly, Matthew shattered the whole calming atmosphere.

'You know,' he began contemplatively, 'he reminds me of someone.'

'Who does?' she sought elucidation warily.

'Steele Cunningham,' he realised her worst fears. Deep creases ridged his forehead as he tried to force recollection. 'But for the life of me I can't think who it is he reminds me of.'

Ravelle knew all too well who it was—Samara—and a suffocating panic gripped her at the idea of him coming to the same conclusion. 'One of the men who works in the mill, perhaps?' she deliberately tried to steer him in the wrong direction, but in a voice she couldn't keep from shaking.

Luckily, that quaver did at least serve to divert his attention, for he leant towards her thoughtfully. 'Are you positive you're all right? You don't sound the best. Maybe you've got a touch of heat exhaustion. I'll go and see if Erin can make up an ice pack for you,' he proposed, jumping to his feet.

'Oh, of course I haven't got heat exhaustion!' she denied in wry exasperation, and without a single tremor. Mental exhaustion, perhaps, from parrying Steele's verbal thrusts, but certainly not of any other kind. 'I was hardly out in the sun at all today. It was just getting a little stuffy in the dining room, that's all.'

'Nonetheless, I still think an ice pack wouldn't go amiss,' Matthew insisted. 'Mother always contends you should start medication at the very first symptom of any ailment, and look what wonders she's wrought with my family's delicately balanced constitutions.'

Wonders! Ravelle almost expostulated aloud. The only thing his mother had done was to turn them all into hypochondriacs who sought their beds the minute they felt the slightest ache or twinge!

'Except that I don't happen to have an ailment,' she protested, but found herself talking to thin air and her fiancé already starting back towards the restaurant. 'Matthew!' she promptly called after him on a pleading note—right at the moment she needed supportive company rather than an ice pack—but there was no response and he continued on into the building.

With a sigh she leant back in her chair and closed her eyes, willing herself to think of anything other than Steele's barbed remarks. At this rate she would be a nervous wreck by the time their holiday came to an end! She was just going to have to adopt a less defensive role, that was all.

The sound of approaching footsteps had her eyes springing open again swiftly, to alight on Vance's tall form as he took the seat next to her.

'Matthew tells us you've got a case of heat exhaustion,' he relayed somewhat quizzically. 'Erin's with him now making up an ice pack for you.'

Ravelle's glance went skywards. 'Oh, it's nothing of the sort,' she discounted. 'And I'm sorry he's troubling Erin unnecessarily, I told him I didn't need one.' Her eyes met his selfconsciously. 'I'm also sorry that we seem to have done nothing *but* cause you trouble ever since we arrived.'

Vance's lips crooked wryly. 'Although in that regard something tells me the traffic hasn't altogether been one way.'

'You mean . . . Steele?' She didn't bother to pretend she didn't know what he was talking about.

'I mean Steele,' he verified drily. 'Of course you can tell me it's none of my business if you like, but would I be right in assuming it was something my brother said, or implied, that made you blanch in the restaurant—not the warmth of the room?'

'I—er . . .' She focussed her gaze on the centre of the table and hunched one shoulder awkwardly. 'Was it that obvious?' she asked in dispirited tones.

'Apparently not to your fiancé,' he half smiled. 'Neither do I think Erin or Chantal realised. Steele no doubt did, but then that's not surprising since I suspect his sole intention was to bait you, and as for myself . . . well, Steele's whole attitude since your and Matthew's arrival has been unusual enough to have me paying more attention to his comments than I would perhaps otherwise have done.'

'And you'd like to know the reason why,' Ravelle surmised. She didn't blame him, so would she if it was her resort which was being disrupted in such a fashion.

Now it was his turn to shrug. 'I wouldn't say no to an explanation if it was on offer.'

Bewilderment was evident in her glance as her troubled eyes rose to his. 'Would you believe, I don't have one to offer because I just *don't know* why?'

'You can't be serious!'

'It is quite unbelievable, isn't it?' She caught her bottom lip between pearly white teeth to still its trembling.

'You mean, you honestly have no idea what could have caused him to act this way?'

Not trusting herself to speak, she shook her head hurriedly. In her opinion the shoe was rightfully entitled to be on the other foot!

With his forehead creased in thought Vance pulled a packet of cigarettes from his shirt pocket, lit one, and began drawing on it absently. Then, intercepting Ravelle's unguarded expression, he smiled apologetically and offered the packet to her.

'It's times like these you need one,' he declared whimsically.

'I guess so,' she acceded, taking one, and thanking him as he applied a lighter flame to its tip. 'Disappointingly, it doesn't provide a solution to my present problem, though.'

Vance was silent for a time, but when he did begin to speak it was in a diffident manner, as if he wasn't too sure of his ground. 'Once again, tell me to go to hell if I'm treading where I shouldn't, but I get the impression from some of Steele's remarks that . . .' He halted, looking uncomfortable, then half smiled contritely and probed, 'Does he know something you would rather Matthew wasn't told?'

She nodded embarrassedly, her cheeks warming under his intent regard.

'And he's blackmailing you with the knowledge?' Vance couldn't keep the stunned incredulity out of his voice.

'N-not really,' she rejected his claim with a frown. Blackmailers usually wanted something in return, didn't they? And Steele had made it all too clear there was nothing else he wanted from her after their last night aboard ship. 'He—he hasn't even mentioned it to me, actually. It was just that, for a moment there, I thought he was intending to deliberately say something that would arouse Matthew's suspicions.'

'Yet you still claim that this—this incident has nothing to do with his attitude towards you?'

Ravelle drew meditatively on her cigarette. 'I don't see how it could have. It wasn't detrimental to him in any way. Quite the reverse, in fact.' An oblique smile passed fleetingly across her lips and she uttered a faint sigh. 'I think you're going to have to ask your brother if you want an answer to this particular riddle. He appears to be the only one who knows what's at the bottom of it.'

'You're not going to ask him yourself?'

'I wouldn't give him the satisfaction! In any case, he seems to be deriving such an amount of sardonic amusement from his goading that I doubt he'd tell me.'

'Hmm, in this instance I guess I'd have to say you could be right,' he granted reluctantly. 'And that's precisely what I find so confusing about all of this. It's so out of character for Steele to act in such a manner.

Normally, he's one of the most straightforward people I
know. If something's riling him, he lets you know, he
doesn't keep you in suspense while he plays cat and
mouse for his own private amusement.'

Then maybe it was just his way of exacting a little
revenge, reasoned Ravelle bitterly. She hadn't made it
easy for Steele's conscience by refusing his cheque, so he
wasn't going to make it easy for her now. Not that she
could say as much to Vance and she let his remarks pass
with a non-committal hunching of one shoulder. Hopefully, once this evening was concluded, she wouldn't be
required to spend any more time in Steele's company
and, consequently, he would be denied the chance to
continue his taunting.

CHAPTER FIVE

HOWEVER, the evening wasn't over yet, and when
Matthew returned with Erin they were also accompanied
by Steele and Chantal—much to Ravelle's dismay. It
appeared her departure from the restaurant hadn't
provided her with a means of escape after all, but merely
occasioned the substitution of one venue for another.

'Here's your ice pack,' announced Erin with a
searching smile. 'How are you feeling now?'

Ravelle accepted the cloth covered bag ruefully. 'Much
better, thank you, although I'm sorry you've been put to
such trouble. I'm sure I haven't got heat exhaustion,'
she disclaimed, and sent her fiancé a chiding look as he
took the seat on her left.

'No, I must admit I didn't really think you would
have,' Erin agreed, sinking into the chair her husband
had just vacated in order to fetch a few others. 'But it was

warm inside tonight, and it might have helped, so I made one up anyway. It was no bother.'

Reaching across the table, Chantal picked up the bag almost as soon as Ravelle put it down. 'Well, if you don't want it, I won't say no,' she declared, putting it to her forehead. A blissful smile came over her features. 'Oh, that's lovely! Just what I needed to prepare me for a spot of dancing. Did I hear you ask me?' she smiled invitingly at the grey-eyed man beside her.

Steele grinned indulgently, and disconcerted Ravelle by the way her senses leapt involuntarily in response. 'If that's what you wish, little one,' he acquiesced amiably. Lithely gaining his feet, he relieved her of the ice pack and replaced it on the table. 'It will be my pleasure.'

With a self-satisfied smile, Chantal was on her feet immediately. 'I won't forget to ask them to play some slower numbers for you either, Matthew, so make certain you join in,' she urged girlishly as they headed for the dance floor.

'How about you, Ravelle? Do you feel up to a little dancing yet?' Vance enquired politely.

'Not just at the moment, thank you,' she declined, shaking her head. Then, keeping up the pretence of having felt off colour for the other two, 'It might be advisable if I wait with Matthew until they play something slower. You and Erin go ahead if you want to, though.'

'You're sure you don't mind?' Erin sought to make certain after she had affirmed the unspoken question asked by her husband's raised brows.

'No, that's all right.' It was Matthew who answered. 'I'm inclined to think Ravelle shouldn't be dancing at all this evening. It may not have been heat exhaustion,' he admitted with patent unwillingness, 'but she didn't look at all well when we left the restaurant. In fact, I'm of the opinion she should call it a night right now and get as much rest as possible . . . just in case.'

Erin and Vance promptly made to resume their seats, and it was only after Ravelle had convinced them she wouldn't be doing any such thing that they finally consented to join the dancing themselves.

'For heaven's sake, Matthew, you make it sound as if I've contracted some debilitating disease!' she rounded on him irritably as soon as their hosts were out of earshot. 'I felt a little faint for a moment, nothing more, but I'm perfectly okay now, I can assure you.'

'You yourself said you thought it advisable to wait until the band played something slower, so you can't have recovered completely,' he stated in somewhat triumphant-sounding tones.

'Only because I didn't want Erin and Vance thinking they had to keep us company,' she evaded hastily. 'Furthermore, if Chantal does persuade the band to play the type of music you prefer, is it so surprising that I would rather wait until then and dance with my fiancé?'

Matthew's countenance took on a considerably less dour expression. 'Of course not,' he was more than willing to agree. 'Provided you're absolutely certain you do feel up to it.'

'Oh, I think I'll be able to manage a few turns around the floor without coming apart at the seams,' she smiled banteringly.

A statement she had cause to revise some minutes later when, apparently at Chantal's request, the style of music did change to a more leisurely tempo and Matthew finally condescended to take part in the dancing with the rest of the guests. It seemed they'd barely had time to complete one circumnavigation of the patio before they noticed Chantal urging Steele alongside them.

'Change partners!' the shapely redhead proposed gaily, to Ravelle's horror, and had insinuated herself into Matthew's arms with a sensuous wiggle before the taller girl could register an objection. 'It's only fair that you give me at least one dance, Matthew, in repayment for my efforts on your behalf,' she claimed, her eyes gazing winsomely into his.

'Ef-efforts on m-my behalf?' Matthew stammered, reddening. He wasn't used to attractive females showing such an interest in him, nor to those who stood so close he could feel every curve of their outline pressed against him.

'For the change in pace,' she explained with a laugh. 'You surely don't begrudge me a dance in exchange, do you? Ravelle won't mind.' She cast a roguish glance over her shoulder to where the younger girl was standing almost open-mouthed in disbelief and indignation. 'Will you?'

'Well, as a matter of fact, I . . .'

'You see, I told you she wouldn't,' Chantal cut in before Ravelle could go any farther. 'So come on and don't be such a stick-in-the-mud.' She began edging him away determinedly.

Weakly allowing himself to be overcome, Matthew directed Ravelle an apologetic half smile. 'I—I'll be back shortly,' he advised rather sheepishly.

Ravelle's acknowledgment was merely an infuriated glare, and then she swung to face the man standing silently beside her.

'I suppose I have you to thank for that . . .' she pressed her lips together angrily '. . . that nauseating little charade, do I?' she blazed.

Ash-coloured eyes ranged coolly over her upturned face. 'Sorry to disappoint you, but no, that was all Chantal's own work.' His mouth shaped mockingly, hatefully. 'You overestimate your charms, honey, if you think it was a burning desire on my part to dance with you that caused that charade, as you call it.'

Vivid scarlet scalded her cheeks at the disparaging inflection in his voice, but refusing to drop her gaze, she forced herself to eye him back with equal sarcasm. 'Then you won't object if I take my leave, will you? because I've no wish to dance with you either, Steele Cunningham!' she retaliated.

'But you will anyway, if only for appearances' sake!' An inflexible hand trapped her wrist in a bone-crushing grip as she about-faced and spun her back into inescapable arms. 'You and your fiancé have already created more disturbances than your importance warrants since almost the first minute you set foot on the island.'

'*We've* created disturbances!' she spluttered incredulously, her hands coming up to his chest in an attempt to push herself away from him. 'Don't you think it would be a trifle more honest if you admitted *you* created them?'

Steele threw back his head and laughed, sardonically. 'Look who's talking about honesty!' he countered on a jeering note. 'After the way you've obviously pulled the wool over poor Matthew's eyes too!'

'Don't you give me "poor Matthew", you couldn't care less about him! And—and whatever I did before I met him is none of his business,' she contended, albeit a little shakily.

Capturing her right hand in his left, Steele swept her close against his rugged form with his right arm, compelling her to keep step with him as he began to move to the music. 'Especially when he's such a puritan character, hmm?' he gibed.

'That has nothing to do with it! Not that he is a—a puritan, of course,' Ravelle amended breathlessly. The feel of his hand on her bare back and his muscular thighs pressing against hers with every move they took was producing a capricious awareness within her which was completely disorganising her thoughts.

'No?' One expressive brow quirked upwards satirically. 'Well, what would you call it then when he not only disapproves of smoking and drinking—even in moderation—but, according to you, he also avoids making love as well?'

'That isn't what I said!' she denied hoarsely.

'You mean he has made love to you?'

'No!' She shook her head wildly, straining futilely to escape his hold. 'But that doesn't . . .'

'What a waste!' In a sense it was a compliment, but Ravelle didn't see it that way as it came slicing drily into her attempted explanation. 'Maybe I should drop a hint in his ear as to what he's missing. Do you suppose that would bring about a more loving reaction?'

'Stop it, stop it!' she choked, close to tears. That Steele should try to cheapen the feelings she'd had for him to such an extent was more than she could bear. 'You have no right to say such things. Why should it matter to you what I tell Matthew, or what his reactions are?'

'For the moment, let's just say I feel for him, knowing he's putting his faith in the wrong person,' he taunted.

'You! Feel for him?' she echoed scornfully. 'I doubt if you've ever felt for anyone but yourself in your whole life!'

'Unlike your so very understanding husband, eh?'

The sudden switch in the conversation had Ravelle struggling desperately to rally her defences. Where Steele was concerned this was her most dangerous ground and she couldn't afford to make even the smallest mistake.

'Tell me,' he continued musingly, 'when did you meet this paragon?'

'Some months before I went to Japan,' she replied stiffly.

'Yet, as I recall, there was no talk of a coming marriage when I met you.'

She shrugged with pseudo-nonchalance, not giving him the satisfaction of knowing his callous desertion had caused her any heartbreak. 'It hardly seemed appropriate to mention it at the time.'

His eyes narrowed fractionally. 'But in due course you became a picture-book bride in *virginal* white,' he derided in corrosive accents.

'Something like that,' she nodded discomfitedly, her face flaming anew as a result of his pungent emphasis. She scanned the other dancers frantically. Why on earth hadn't Matthew come to reclaim her? Surely he had finished his dance with Chantal by now!

'After tumbling straight out of my bed into his, I presume?'

'No!' Her retort came resentfully while her thoughts were still engaged with Matthew's non-appearance. 'Not that it's any concern of yours, in any case! So if you don't mind, I'd appreciate it if you'd just forget the subject. As I told you this afternoon, I find it very upsetting to talk about that period of my life,' she finished with creditable calm.

'Yeah, I'm sure you must . . . as *I* told *you* this afternoon,' he ground out, his eyes as cold and hard as chips of ice. 'And especially when you have a daughter who was obviously conceived *before* any such marriage could have taken place!'

If Ravelle's face had been brightly tinted before, every scrap of colour drained from it now as her heart skipped a beat, then raced on thunderously. 'Wh-what makes you think that?' she gasped, stalling for time in which to recover her wits.

Steele's head inclined menacingly near. 'An ability to add!' he enlightened with grating sarcasm. 'As any cattleman can tell you, the gestation period for both cows and humans is nearly identical, and therefore, if one knows the date of conception it's a relatively simple matter to predict within almost a couple of days when birth is likely to occur.'

He was too perilously close to the mark and she tried bluffing her way out. 'Yes, well, that's very interesting, b-but I fail to see what that has to—to do with me.'

'Your daughter's date of birth—kindly provided by your fiancé—just about coincides *to the day* with conception having taken place that last night aboard the *Capricornia*, Ravelle!' he elucidated harshly.

If he hadn't been holding her so tightly Ravelle was certain her shaking limbs would never have been able to support her, but even despite her trembling she made herself take the last chance left to her.

'You think Sam might be *your* child?' she half laughed on a hollow, breaking note. 'Th-that's r-ridiculous! She was—she was born more than a month prematurely.'

'You lying little bitch!' he exploded savagely. 'Do you really expect me to believe that when you not only sound as guilty as hell, but you look it as well?'

'I don't care what you believe! Samara isn't yours!' she cried almost hysterically. Oh, God, where *was* Matthew?

'That being the case, you won't have any objection to my checking the appropriate State registers for information relating to both her birth *and* your supposed marriage, will you?' he bit out fiercely from between tightly clamped teeth.

Too agitated now to even continue her pretence at dancing, Ravelle started to fight against him in panic. 'Leave me alone! I hate you! My life's nothing to do with you! Sam's mine, not yours!' she sobbed incoherently.

Conscious that some curious glances were being aimed their way by those dancers closest to them, Steele swiftly propelled her struggling form into the darkness provided by the clustered trees that lined one side of the patio, and followed the path on the other side until they reached the deserted beach.

Once there, he finally released her, and making the most of the opportunity Ravelle immediately turned and began to run back the way they had come. Her high heels, however, weren't made for use on such an unstable footing and she had only managed to stagger a few steps before Steele caught hold of her and swung her around to face him again.

'You're not going anywhere until I say so!' he snapped, his fingers ruining her carefully controlled french pleat as they sank roughly within her hair. 'Now, do I check those registers or not? Believe me, it's not hard to do, and the company has a lawyer in Sydney who can have the information radioed back to me within a matter of hours.'

Ravelle closed her eyes disconsolately, her teeth gnawing worriedly at her lips. It wasn't fair that everything should always go his way, she railed despairingly.

'Well?' he demanded impatiently.

She gave in helplessly, defeatedly. 'All right, all right, it's true.'

'What is, Ravelle?' He shook her sharply. 'I want to hear you say it.'

She moved her head from side to side in disbelief. 'Oh, God, you're a cruel swine! Isn't it enough for you that I've admitted it?'

'No, it's not! I want it spelt out by your own lips, just so there can be no mistake. So, whose daughter is she?' he cued.

'Yours ... Sam's your daughter,' she confessed tremulously. Anguished brown eyes sought his through a tearful blur. 'Now may I leave?'

Steele gave a staccato bark of humourless laughter. 'No way! I'm not through with you yet by any means!'

'I—I don't understand.'

'You will by the time I'm finished!'

The sheer vehemence in his voice was sufficient to have Ravelle shivering uncontrollably. 'Please, Steele, there's nothing more to tell,' she whispered.

'By you? Not much, I agree,' his affirmation came with icy grimness. 'But you can rest assured there's quite a deal I'll be telling you.'

'A-about what?'

'All in good time. Why rush to hear bad news?' he mocked.

Fear of what he intended had her eyes turning black in the moonlight and she swallowed heavily. 'What bad news?' she questioned apprehensively.

With her anxiety drawing her to him like a magnet there was no necessity for Steele to continue holding her captive, and with a careless hunching of broad shoulders he set her free. But he mercilessly ignored her tormented question.

'You weren't ever married either, were you, Ravelle?' he probed instead.

'No,' she sighed cursorily. At the moment she wasn't even concerned enough to ask how he had come by that deduction. Maybe it had merely been as a result of his other discovery. She didn't really care. Her only interest was in gaining an answer to the query she now repeated. 'What bad news, Steele?'

'Can't you guess?' he drawled goadingly, completely in command now.

'N-no.'

'I want my daughter!' she was informed with stony determination, all signs of mockery disappearing.

'*No!*' There was nothing hesitant in the word when she uttered it this time. It was a protesting cry made in terror. 'She's mine! You can't mean it!'

'The hell I can't!' he snarled. 'If for no other reason than that there's no way on this damned earth I'm having that miserable excuse for a man, Matthew Inglis, rearing any child of mine! I could kill you just for considering that alone, Ravelle!'

It was doubtful if she heard him. 'Oh, please, Steele, don't do this for revenge!' she begged tearfully. Never did she doubt for one moment that should there be any legal obstacles to prevent him from taking Samara away from her they would somehow be swiftly and assiduously overcome. He had *that* much of his father's ruthlessness in him!

'I would hardly call it vengeful to want my daughter to have all the advantages I can give her,' he countered tersely.

'But there's more to bringing up a child than the provision of material assets,' she cried. 'There's love, and caring, and—and just being there. Oh, Steele, she's little more than a baby. She needs her mother!'

'But, judging by your attempts at secrecy, not her father, is that it?'

A spark of resentment flared. 'I wasn't to know you'd care whether we had a child or not!'

'Then perhaps you should have taken the trouble to find out!' he rasped caustically. 'And while we're on the subject—just to put the record straight—I'm no less capable of giving my daughter all the love and care she needs than you are, believe me. Likewise, on the matter of "being there", I think you'll find I can fulfil that requirement to an even greater extent than you can.'

'By taking her into conference rooms with you, and—and dragging her all over the country on your business trips?' she challenged desolately.

The crooked curve to his lips was disdainful. 'Not at all. Fortunately, if and when the necessity arises, I'm able to delegate most of the work which would take me away from home. Can you say the same with regard to yours?'

Ravelle didn't even attempt to try. 'My p-parents are

very willing stand-ins,' she offered dejectedly in lieu.

'As I'm sure my mother will be too.'

Tears began to spill from the corners of her eyes. Nothing she said was making the slightest impression on him and the knowledge was ripping her insides to shreds. Ramrod-stiff, she risked a threat as a last resort.

'I won't stand idly by if you do try and take her away from me, Steele,' she warned in a low poignant voice. 'Before I let that happen I'll take her away myself to—to some place where you'll never find her.'

'You think not?' A nerve along his jawline tensed, and his eyes glittered wrathfully. 'However, thanks to your forewarning, that won't be necessary, will it?' He grasped her about the chin with a forceful hand. 'In fact, in order to ensure your cheap little threat doesn't eventuate, it might even be worth my while to arrange for Samara's removal to my home before you leave Morning Retreat, mightn't it?'

'You wouldn't!' she wept openly, petrified by the thought of him carrying out his threat. 'Oh, no, you couldn't!'

Freeing her, Steele took a couple of paces back along the path. 'Try me!' he turned to recommend implacably over one shoulder.

'Steele, no!' She stumbled frantically after him to clutch beseechingly at his arm. 'You couldn't be so heartless as to uproot her in such an insensitive fashion. She'd be frightened to death at being forced to leave everything she knows so suddenly, while I—while I . . .'

'Mmm?'

'Would be lost without her,' she concluded throatily.

'Then I suggest you quickly marry Matthew and replace her with a couple of his progeny!' he exhorted pitilessly and, shaking her hand away, resumed walking.

Shock and utter despair combined to have Ravelle's

trembling legs refusing to hold her upright any longer, and she sank to her knees in the sand, finally giving way to the racking torrent of sobs which had been threatening for so long as she bowed her head in her hands.

Replace Samara, he had said. Didn't he know he was asking the impossible, or was it that he just didn't care? No child could ever be a substitute for another, and especially not for her adored daughter who was so essentially a part of her, and of . . . *him*! Ravelle's weeping grew more harsh, her slender body heaving convulsively. She had believed her feelings for Steele had died a long time ago—killed by a mixture of defection and starvation—but now she was beginning to realise they had merely been slumbering deep within her, awaiting the chance to spring into overpowering life once again at their first opportunity. It didn't seem to matter to her heart that he was about to make a shambles of her life for the second time. Response to his presence was apparently its only concern, and that she was discovering she was helpless to control.

Choking for breath, she lifted her head slightly, and flinched sharply away on seeing Steele squatting beside her, his hand reaching out to smooth her tousled hair.

'Stop crying like that, Ravelle, you'll make yourself ill,' he sighed.

Fresh shudders wrenched through her, leaving her shaking helplessly. 'A-another s-success for—for you?' she charged jerkily. 'You m-must be q-quite p-pr . . .' Too distraught to continue, she dissolved into another paroxysm of tears, her head drooping forward despondently.

'No, I'm not proud of myself at having brought you to this,' he denied, guessing what she had left unsaid. 'But you can't hide that kind of information from a man and expect to remain unscathed when the truth finally comes out.'

Ravelle didn't reply, she wasn't able to, and when she felt his hands on her arms drawing her closer, she offered only a token resistance before allowing her head to rest weakly against his chest and her storm of crying to expend itself within the circle of his strong arms.

'Here,' he murmured gently a few minutes after her crying had finally ceased, and tilting her face up to his he began drying her cheeks with a handkerchief he took from this pocket. This completed, Ravelle watched sombrely as he replaced the now damp white square, her fingers intertwined tightly.

'Steele . . .' she began unsurely, fastening her gaze to his throat. 'I know I shouldn't have tried keeping Sam a secret from you, but . . .' now her eyes lifted to his, imploringly, '*please* don't take her away from me. I—I love her so much!' A shivering breath escaped her.

He laid a hand against her flushed, still damp cheek. 'That's very apparent, honey, but I'm sorry, I can't change my mind,' he shook his head regretfully. 'I also would like to become acquainted with my daughter, and as I said before, I categorically refuse to have Inglis exerting any influence over her.'

In a last-ditch effort to prevent the inevitable, she was willing to sacrifice anything. 'W-would there be a chance of you reconsidering if—if Matthew didn't have anything to do with her upbringing?' she asked hesitantly.

'How do you mean?' intently.

She sucked in a deep, steadying lungful of air. 'I mean, if I didn't marry him,' she disclosed in a rush.

'You would call off your engagement in order to keep Samara?'

'Yes!' Her endorsement came without delay, or a falter. There was only one person who meant as much to her as her daughter, and that was the man she was with right now!

He flexed his shoulders impassively. 'I still don't think . . .'

'Oh, please don't reject the idea out of hand,' she cut in anxiously, her brain racing to find logical reasons why he should alter his decision. 'You could visit her whenever you wanted to, I wouldn't try and stop you, and—and since you have your own plane you know it would be much easier for you to fly to Wollongong than it would be for me to—to . . .' She came to a trembling halt. Even if she did manage to make it to his property in the outback, she didn't know if she'd be welcome. Unbidden tears washed into her eyes once more at the thought. 'I'm so frightened I'll never see her again if you take her.'

'Of course you'll see her again!' he averred, running a hand distractedly through his hair. 'I just don't . . .' It was a feminine hand that stopped his words this time as Ravelle rushed to still his lips with her fingers lest he was about to utter what she least wanted to hear.

'*Please!*' she entreated again, her gaze clinging piteously to his.

Whether it was the hypnotic effect of his grey eyes, dark and deep as they continued to hold hers, or the touch of his firm mouth against her fingers, Ravelle didn't know, but all of a sudden she felt as if an electric charge had passed through her quivering body and the shock of it kept her staring at him as if frozen. Momentarily, the air between them almost sparked with tension, then, with a deep-pitched groan, Steele dragged her towards him roughly and his lips took possession of hers with a compulsive hunger.

Ravelle's response was instantaneous—an aching desire she couldn't withhold—and she melted against him sinuously, her body aflame, her senses whirling. Beneath his, her lips parted invitingly, opening sweet depths for his willing exploration, while her ranging fingertips rediscovered pleasures of their own as they slid under the silk knit of his shirt to caress the bunching muscles of his broad back.

With a sharply indrawn breath, Steele abruptly thrust her from him. 'God damn you, Ravelle!' he swore explosively. 'You always did set a beguiling trap, but you're not going to catch this male in it again!'

His accusation sliced through her emotionally weakened defences with brutal efficiency, and was reflected in the misty dimming of her eyes. 'I didn't ask you to kiss me,' she reminded him in an unsteady whisper.

To her surprise he laughed at that. But it was in low, self-mocking amusement. 'No, I guess you didn't,' he admitted, exhaling heavily. 'But then you never did have to, did you?'

Ravelle averted her face despairingly. 'And that's just one more reason for taking Samara away, is it?' she deduced miserably. His attitude wasn't a favourable one for the granting of her plea.

'I wasn't aware of having said so,' he returned tautly, levering himself to his feet.

'You are still going to take her, though, aren't you?'

'According to you, I am, it seems.'

According to her? Hope swelled in her heart as she turned her gaze upwards. 'You mean you were re-considering?'

He hunched one shoulder noncommittally and had her expression changing to one of reproach. 'Steele!' she quavered tormentedly.

For his part he half turned away, one hand rubbing at the back of his neck as he lifted his face skywards. 'Okay, *okay*, you can keep her,' he allowed eventually. A proviso quickly followed, however. 'But only on condition you break your engagement to Inglis *before* you leave this island.'

At his change of heart relief flooded through Ravelle

like a river in spate, but before she could express her thankfulness his addition distracted her. 'Oh, but . . .'

'Take it or leave it!' His interrupting ultimatum was adamantly voiced.

Something in his demeanour brought a perplexed look to her eyes. 'You don't trust me to otherwise?' she quizzed curiously.

The cynical upsweep of his shapely mouth was a sufficient answer without his sardonic quip, 'You guessed!'

'But that wasn't why . . .'

'I said, take it or leave it, Ravelle!'

'Well, naturally I'll take it,' she accepted hurriedly. His warning tone didn't exactly encourage any delay. 'And I—I'm very grateful that you altered your decision, of course. It's just that, with regard to Matthew . . .'

'Quite frankly, I don't give a damn about Matthew!' he cut bitingly into her attempted explanation once more.

'More than likely, but I do,' she returned earnestly. 'In his way he's been good to both Sam and me these last couple of years, and I don't want to hurt his feelings any more than I have to.'

'Your emotions not being at risk, presumably, by the readiness with which you're willing to give him up?' he gibed.

A light flush lent her cheeks a rosy glow. 'I shall miss his company, of course, but Samara will always be my first consideration,' she relayed stiffly.

'Always?' One eyebrow winged its way upwards expressively.

'Yes, always!' she reiterated a little fierily. She would never give him another excuse for taking her daughter from her. 'And just because I've agreed to your condition, Steele, don't think that means you have the right to make fun of Matthew's and my relationship. That isn't any of your business.'

'Except for deciding when you'll put an end to your little twosome, don't forget,' he smiled aggravatingly.

'Which is just what I wanted to discuss with you.' She pounced on the opportunity rapidly. 'Don't you see, if I break our engagement while we're still here, then it's highly probable Matthew will become extremely suspicious of my reasons.'

'So? That's your problem, honey, not mine.'

'As long as it doesn't become Samara's too!' she retorted as she scrambled upright.

That put a halt to his somewhat facetious amusement. 'Go on,' he prompted watchfully.

'I—well, he's already made the comment that you remind him of someone, but as yet he hasn't realised who it is . . . fortunately.' She moved restlessly beneath his alert scrutiny, her own eyes dropping selfconsciously. 'Sam's—er—very like you in a lot of ways.'

Steele digested the information dispassionately. 'And?'

'Well, if he does come to the conclusion that you're her father then he'll know she's illegitimate!'

'In other words, it's your own skin you're worried about for having deceived him all this time with that fake marriage of yours!' he condemned contemptuously.

'No!' Ravelle shook her head vigorously. 'I can take care of myself, but Sam wouldn't understand, and I'm concerned that Matthew might, in a fit of pique if he should discover the truth . . .'

'Start telling tales out of school, as it were?' he finished for her.

'Something like that,' she agreed reluctantly.

'Then before he leaves here, I shall just have to take him to one side and quietly explain the inadvisability of such an action, won't I?' he proposed with inflexible resolve. 'In any case, there's bound to be at least some talk when Samara changes her name from Fenton to Cunningham.'

Ravelle promptly forgot her dismay at the thought of what he might say to Matthew in order to exclaim, aghast, 'Changes her name! Are you mad? That's almost the same as Matthew telling everyone! Why ever is that necessary?'

'Because I'm not so understanding as your make-believe husband was,' he drawled mockingly. 'My daughter will carry *my* name—no one else's—and especially as I intend to be the one supporting her.'

Unaccountably, his claim reminded her of the last time he'd offered her money, and resentment prickled at the memory. 'Oh, do you? Just like that, eh?' she smouldered. 'Well, let me tell you something, Steele Cunningham! It may have been a struggle at times, but I've managed to support *my* daughter quite satisfactorily until now, thanks very much, and I don't need any charity from you to continue doing so!'

'Charity?' For a moment he looked taken aback as he stared at her from under lowering brows. 'That's ridiculous, and you know it! What's more, no matter what you choose to call it, you will accept maintenance for her, Ravelle, make no mistake about that!'

'I see,' she muttered rebelliously. 'In return for being allowed custody of my own daughter, I'm to give up all other rights concerning her from now on, is that it?'

Steele lifted his hands to rest them on lithe hips, his head bending forward slightly in a cautioning manner, yet with a contradictory smile pulling at his lips. 'Honey, don't give me reason to regret changing my mind tonight, or you may really find your rights being ignored,' he counselled lazily. 'Instead, why don't you just devote your time and energies to breaking your engagement to Inglis with as little fuss as possible, hmm?'

Ravelle glared at him impotently. Now that he knew Samara was his daughter he would always be in a position to enforce his dictates with the threat of her removal, she fumed. As for Matthew—well . . . .

'That could be easier said than done,' she grimaced. 'Matthew isn't the type to take rejection lightly, I'm afraid.'

His mouth twisted sarcastically. 'Your concern for his feelings touches me, but you'll still tell him before you leave here . . . or else!'

'All right, all right,' she flared. 'But I'll do it in my own time and in my own way, without any hints from you, understand?'

'He's your fiancé,' he shrugged indifferently. 'If I never speak to him again I'm not likely to lose any sleep over it.'

And why would he? she asked herself sourly. So far everything had played into his hands very nicely!

CHAPTER SIX

RAVELLE didn't wake the next morning until a knock on her door heralded the arrival of her breakfast tray—Matthew having had his and left on his arranged fishing trip an hour or so earlier—and although she would normally have preferred to have her meal in the dining room instead of being incarcerated on her own, this particular morning she was grateful for the seclusion it afforded. No doubt Steele would have regaled Vance and Erin, and probably Chantal as well, with the full facts regarding Samara's parenthood, and she felt somewhat uncomfortable at the thought of what their reaction to the news was likely to be.

Consequently, she took her time over eating and after a leisurely wash donned an orange and black patterned bikini which complemented the honey gold tones of her already tanned skin and prepared to head for the beach. Naturally enough, the garment wasn't one which found favour in Matthew's eyes. A less revealing one-piece swimsuit was his idea of the only suitable beachwear for a female—and probably only of the neck-to-knee kind, Ravelle had often surmised wryly—but to his unconcealed annoyance, her style of dress was one matter she had steadfastly refused to let him direct, although it was still a relief to know that because of his absence there would be no recriminations levelled at her attire for at least today.

Of course, she recalled with a sigh, very shortly he would have no right to censure her in any regard whatsoever, and as she made her way beneath the swaying palms to the warm inviting sand her thoughts returned to her most pressing problem.

Just how was she going to gently, but decisively, break her engagement to Matthew without giving him a hint as to the real reason?

Spreading out her towel some distance from those other guests already soaking up the sunshine, Ravelle sank down on to it absently, to sit with her hands linked about her updrawn knees as she gazed unseeingly at the green slopes of Hermitage across the way.

As she had told Steele the previous evening, she knew her fiancé well enough to know he wouldn't accept being jilted quietly, or with dignity. His immediate reaction, she had no doubt, would be unadulterated anger, swiftly followed by a suspicious interrogation as to the whys and wherefores of her decision, and especially the motive which prompted her to make the break during their holiday! Her teeth tugged worriedly at her soft underlip. It would all have been so much more simple if Steele hadn't insisted on her ties with Matthew being severed while they were still on the island.

As it was, no matter what reason she offered for her decision she guessed her fiancé wouldn't be satisfied with it—except for the truth, of course, and it was doubtful if *satisfied* would be the most apt description for his reaction to that discovery!—and since that was the last thing she wanted him to know, it left her in something of a quandary as to how best to convince him nothing, or perhaps more relevantly, *no one* on the island had influenced her change of heart.

Ravelle wasn't certain for how long she sat pondering the various excuses she might reasonably present to Matthew, but she gathered it must have been quite some time, because it wasn't until two young boys came bursting through the undergrowth directly behind her that her attention was distracted. Exact duplicates of one another, it wasn't difficult to figure whose sons they were, although had she not known differently, she would have put their ages closer to twelve than to ten, for they were both well above average size.

Only just managing to miss tumbling over her they came to an abrupt halt with their dark curly heads lowering sheepishly and their deep blue eyes filled with a combination of laughter and contrition.

'Sorry,' mumbled one ruefully. 'Did we frighten you?'

'No, you just took me by surprise, that's all,' Ravelle disclaimed with a reassuring smile. 'I wasn't expecting anyone to suddenly appear out of the bushes like that.'

The one who had spoken looked to his brother and grinned. 'We didn't think anybody would be here. Mostly everyone stays down there.' He pointed towards the more populated part of the beach in front of the resort.

'While you prefer to explore a little farther afield?' she smiled.

'We know all the best places on *both* islands,' the other half of the pair now chimed in proudly. 'We live here all the time, you know.'

Ravelle nodded her acknowledgment. 'And your names are Dion and Craig.'

'How did you know that?' he frowned.

'Probably 'cos someone told her, stupid,' the first one retorted with brotherly disparagement. 'Didn't they?' he sought confirmation from Ravelle.

'Yes, your mother, as a matter of fact,' she endorsed, looking laughingly from one to the other. 'She also said I'd have trouble telling you apart, and she's right, so I'll have to rely on you to tell me which of you is which.'

'Oh, that's easy, I'm Dion,' said the second one.

'No, he's not, I am,' the other promptly contradicted, eyes shining mischievously.

It was obviously a game they enjoyed playing and without the additional knowledge Erin had given her, Ravelle suspected it might have been some considerable time before they willingly revealed their true identities. But she wasn't above playing tricks herself and, assuming a mystic mien, she studied each of their sturdy brown bodies in turn for those telltale distinguishing scars.

'I see,' she finally pretended to muse, tapping a forefinger to her chin. 'Then I suppose I shall just have to get you to sit beside me so I can put my hands on your heads and see what signals your personal vibrations transmit, shan't I?'

They were on their knees in the sand almost before she had finished speaking. 'Can you really do that?' asked the first, the one she now knew to be Dion, in eager anticipation.

'I'll certainly try,' she claimed with twitching lips as she rested a hand on each of their heads.

'Is anything happening, is anything happening?' Craig repeated himself in his enthusiasm for the experiment.

'Mmm—yes, I think I'm getting something. It's a letter. A—a letter C. You're Craig!' she announced in positive tones. She turned to the boy on her right. 'And you're Dion!'

'But—but how did you do it?' they stuttered almost in unison.

'Simple,' she shrugged nonchalantly, then confessed with a chuckle, 'The more so after I'd located the scar,' she patted Dion on the arm, 'you have on your hand, and the one,' she did the same to Craig's leg, 'you have on your knee.'

For a few seconds they stared at her blankly, but as soon as they realised she had been playing a joke on them their mouths split into wide identical grins and they doubled over in bouts of childish laughter.

'You knew all the time,' accused Dion, still giggling.

'Not really,' she smiled. 'At least, not until I'd had a good search for those scars.'

'We didn't think Mum would've told you about them,' beamed Craig unashamedly.

'So I gathered.' Ravelle eyed them with mock severity.

Seemingly in no hurry to move on, Dion rolled over on to his stomach and propped himself up on his elbows, his head tilting quizzically. 'Are you a friend of Mum's, then?'

'Not really,' she denied again. 'I only met her for the first time yesterday, actually, but we just happened to be discussing our respective children at dinner last night and she mentioned the ways in which it was becoming easier to tell you two apart.'

'Oh.' He nodded his comprehension, then enquired, 'How many children have you got?'

'Only one. A little girl, but she was too young to come to the island.'

Once more he nodded, but this time followed it with a searching look up and down the beach. 'Are you here on your own?'

'Well, I am for today,' she revealed wryly. 'Matthew—

the man I came with—has gone on a fishing trip.'

'With Dad and some others to Tern Cay,' put in Craig knowledgeably.

'That's right.'

'Didn't you want to go?' Dion was the one with all the questions.

Ravelle moved one shoulder slightly, her mouth curving ruefully. If she remembered correctly, Matthew hadn't even bothered to enquire. 'No, I thought I might do a little exploring round here instead.'

'We could show you some of Hermitage, if you like,' offered Craig generously. 'We've got to go over to pick up some mangoes for Mum before lunch.'

'Mmm, and it's nicer when the tide's over the causeway. There's not so many people around,' added his brother expressively.

Since she was also one of those same people they apparently felt disturbed the island's tranquillity, Ravelle supposed the twins were doing her an honour in suggesting she accompany them and she accepted the invitation with pleasure. Besides, she reasoned to herself, they probably knew both islands better than anyone else and, for all she knew, by the time Matthew got around to taking his guided tour of the other island they might not even be on speaking terms and she could miss out altogether.

Presently, after having returned to her cabin in order to wrap a matching skirt over her bikini pants and to slip her feet into low-heeled sandals, Ravelle rejoined her escorts at the beach where they had already pushed a fibreglass runabout into the water.

Fortunately, from Ravelle's point of view, the twins were far more conversant with outboards than she was, and after a hefty pull on the starter cord Dion soon had the little craft heading smoothly across the inlet. Below them vivid marine life darted through the unbelievably clear water, and with Craig conscientiously pointing out the various species of fish as they flashed past it was with regret that she saw the waters shallow and heard the grating of sand against the hull as Dion beached and competently moored the boat.

From the shoreline Hermitage seemed even larger than it had from Hideaway and scanning the rather steeply rising slope before her, Ravelle's finely marked brows lifted explicitly at the thought of having to make it to the top on foot. To her relief, she soon found that wasn't necessary because there was a steel shed located to the right of the path they followed between the overhanging trees which housed half a dozen or so mokes, and it was to one of these that her companions directed her. Appearing as used to driving these little vehicles as they were to managing runabouts, it didn't take long for Craig to have them in motion and making effortlessly for the top of the hill.

'Good lord!' The exclamation was forced involuntarily from Ravelle's lips as they came out on to a high grassed plateau which spread almost the length and breadth of the island. 'It never occurred to me that it would be like this up here, or that the place was quite this large.' Although she had known it was much longer than Hideaway, she hadn't realised just how wide it was as well. 'And look at that view! It's out of this world!' she went on enthusiastically, glancing across the lushly green paddocks to the cobalt sea beyond where waves rippled whitely against the barrier of the surrounding reef.

Since it had been their suggestion to show her the island Dion and Craig now puffed up with pride at her show of obvious appreciation as if they had personally created the scene before them, and all too eager to point out the various places of interest the island had to offer.

'Down there's Mariner Bay,' Dion leant forward from the back seat to indicate a cove nestling in the lee of a rounded promontory. 'It's one of the best beaches at Morning Retreat.'

'So's its reef,' added Craig with relish. 'It's not as large as the one round Hideaway, but the coral's really great.'

'Then out there are the bouncing stones.' Dion pointed to the headland in front of them.

'Bouncing stones?' Ravelle half turned to frown quizzically at him.

'Mmm,' he nodded emphatically. 'You throw them up in the air and they bounce, just like a ball.'

'But only against others of the same kind,' qualified Craig. 'They won't do it against different sorts of rock, or concrete, or anything like that.'

'You're sure you don't mean they skim off each other when you shy them?'

'Uh-uh!' They were both most definite on that point. 'Dad says it's got something to do with energy and that they're a natural phen-phen . . .'

'Phenomenon?' she suggested helpfully.

'That's it,' Dion grinned gratefully. 'We'll take you down to look at them when we get to the house.'

'Would that be the roof you can see among the trees from Hideaway?'

'Yes, that's where Mr and Mrs Baldwin live. He's the manager over here,' he advised informatively. 'Jim, Doug, and Barney, have their own quarters next door. Barney grows most of the fruit and vegetables used in the restaurant, while Jim and Doug look after the stock.'

'Quite a little community, in fact,' Ravelle acknowledged with a smile that froze on her face as two riders suddenly emerged from a stand of trees just ahead of the moke. Their direction was putting them on an intercepting course with the little vehicle somewhere in the vicinity of the fork in the track they were fast approaching.

Ravelle's wayward senses had informed her of the

tallest rider's identity immediately her eyes came to rest on him, and now she began to call herself all manner of fools for having forgotten—owing to her earlier preoccupation as to the best way in which she might break her engagement—that, since Steele had said he was only at Morning Retreat in order to check on their cattle, then it was more than likely he would spend the majority of his time on Hermitage. And his still wasn't a presence she wanted any contact with at the moment!

Although his discovery that Samara was his child might have relieved her of the strain of keeping that particular secret from him, another fear had rapidly, disturbingly, replaced it after that one emotion-charged kiss last night. That he might also discover her feelings towards him were nowhere near as indifferent as she had originally believed, or as she would have liked.

The twins, of course, were burdened with no such problems and began waving and calling as soon as he rode into view. At the turn-off the older, stockier man who was accompanying him gave a casual acknowledging salute in the moke's general direction and, with a few last smiling words, continued down the track which Ravelle guessed would eventually lead him to the house. In the meantime, Steele brought his chestnut-coloured mount to a halt and resting one hand on a hard thigh waited for the vehicle to pull up beside him.

'Hi, Uncle Steele,' grinned Craig almost before he had turned off the ignition. 'We've come to collect some mangoes for Mum, so we asked—we asked . . .' Faltering to a stop, he sent Ravelle a discomfited, apologetic glance. 'You know our names, but I'm sorry, we didn't ask yours.'

The man seated so indolently on the horse next to them quickly filled him in. 'It's *Ms* Fenton,' he drawled mockingly.

'But you can call me Ravelle,' she promptly counter-

advised the boys determinedly.

They accepted the amendment amiably and Craig continued, 'So we asked Ravelle if she'd like to see some of Hermitage while we were here.'

'I see.' Silver-grey eyes collided with somewhat challenging chocolate brown. 'Then since *personal* guided tours appear to be the in thing at the moment, I guess we'd better ensure we do it in style, hmm?'

'Does that mean you'll come with us?' queried Dion hopefully.

Steele eased forward in his saddle, making the leather creak, his mount dancing a few steps sideways. 'I think perhaps I'd better,' he smiled drily. Facetiously, as far as Ravelle was concerned.

'Oh, no!' The protest slipped from her lips unbidden. Not only was she extremely chary of his company, but she hadn't really appreciated that sniping reference to personal guided tours either! 'I mean, I wouldn't want to interrupt your work, and I'm sure Dion and Craig are quite capable of showing me whatever there is to see.'

'But not, I think, in the time available between now and lunch.'

Ravelle jumped at the excuse indirectly offered. 'Well then, that would seem to settle it,' she shrugged philosophically. 'I'll just have to come back another day to see what the twins haven't time to show me this morning.'

'No, I've got a better idea,' Craig suddenly spoke up with barely contained eagerness. 'Why don't Dion and I take the mangoes back to Hideaway, get Mum to pack us all a picnic lunch, then when we get back we can eat at Mariner Bay.' He smiled at Ravelle encouragingly. 'It's real pretty down there.'

'Yes, I'm sure it is,' she smiled soothingly. 'But I really don't think it's fair to put your mother to all that extra trouble just on my account, and especially when I can come back another time.'

'Oh, but Mum won't mind,' inserted Dion confidently. 'She'll just make up a basket from the food they'll be using in the dining room. Besides,' his dark blue eyes twinkled disarmingly, 'Dad's always saying the staff are only here to serve the guests and make their stay as enjoyable as possible. They packed lunches for all those who went on the fishing trip this morning, so why not for you too?'

A wryly humorous curve had begun to sweep across Steele's lips during the exchange and, noticing it, Ravelle hated the way her heart pounded traitorously in response.

'That—that was for a special reason, though,' she stammered selfconsciously, and trying unsuccessfully to ignore him. 'This isn't, and . . .'

'Oh, please say yes!' Craig broke in to entreat.

'Mmm, it'll be fun,' assured Dion. 'We've only ever shown kids over the island before, never an adult.'

'Neither will you this time if your uncle comes along,' she rushed to point out.

'Uh-uh, they're the guides.' Steele seemed to delight in shooting her argument down in flames. 'I'll just be along for the ride.' One dark brow quirked tauntingly, sardonically. 'Or would you rather I wasn't?'

Of course she would rather he wasn't! As he undoubtedly was very well aware, she seethed. But with the twins looking at her in puzzlement—they weren't to know why she should be so reluctant for his company— and not wanting to give him the satisfaction of forcing her to say so outright, she made herself return his gibing gaze with a calm that was entirely superficial.

'Not at all,' she denied, and pleased that she managed to accompany her words with a lightly amused laugh. 'It makes absolutely no difference to me whether you're with us or not.' Although why he should want to go with them she had no idea.

'Then there's no problem, is there?' Taking her acceptance for granted, he went on to suggest to the twins, 'You boys can leave Ravelle here with me while you collect whatever you need from Barney, and we'll look over the stock-yards, etcetera, until you return.'

Uttering enthusiastic endorsements Craig and Dion waited patiently for their passenger to alight, which she did with the utmost reluctance, and were off in a cloud of dust as soon as she had taken a few steps away from the vehicle.

For a moment she stood watching the moke depart, the palms of her hands absently rubbing their way down the side of her skirt, and then her gaze slanted upwards to the man on her left. It was the first time she had ever seen him in a grazier's typical garb of fawn drills and wide-brimmed hat, and temporarily it distracted her, the more so because he appeared so at home in the saddle—something else she had never before witnessed—and because it seemed to suit him so well. She shook her head quickly to deny the virile attraction he exuded and propelled her thoughts in another direction.

'I thought you said the twins were to be my guides,' she reminded him a little ironically. 'Maybe I should wait until they return before seeing the stockyards.'

Even white teeth showed in a lazy grin. 'Somehow I don't quite think it's the attractions of the yards that they're anxious to show tou,' he drawled. 'In any case, we have to occupy ourselves doing something while we pass the time, and that seemed as good a way as any.' His slate grey eyes slid over her in insolent appraisal. 'Or did you have something more evocative in mind?'

Ravelle flushed, and wished she had worn something a little less revealing, but refused to let him destroy her equanimity altogether. 'No, the yards will be fine,' she answered as matter-of-factly as possible. It seemed the best manner to adopt under the circumstances. 'Whereabouts are they? Down there?' gesturing towards the track the moke had taken.

Steele nodded casually, apparently totally unperturbed by the dispassionateness of her return, and causing Ravelle to speculate bitterly whether he had merely been testing—for his own amusement—to see if she was as willing to succumb to his masculine appeal today as she had been four years ago.

'Do you want to walk or ride?'

His question broke in on her musings, catching her off guard, and making her forget for the moment her unresponsive approach. 'Since you already very well know I can't ride, I'll walk, thanks,' she retorted tartly.

The corners of his mouth twitched annoyingly. 'I hardly think you need to know how to ride just in order to sit behind and hold on,' he declared in chaffing accents.

Hold on to *him*, she presumed. 'I still think I'll walk,' she rejected his suggestion with a sardonic grimace and started off down the sandy track.

The muffled sound of hoofs behind her advised he was following, but she hadn't expected it to be Steele's tall figure which drew alongside her seconds later, his mount trailing after him at the end of the reins, and recovering from her initial surprised look she kept her eyes trained purposefully to the front.

'You don't have to walk just because I am,' she declared in a hopefully rebuffing voice. His proximity was making her distinctly restive. 'After all, you *can* ride.'

With an unconcerned movement of his shoulders he either didn't, or wouldn't, take the hint. Instead, his head angled towards her enquiringly. 'How come, out of all the people staying at the resort, it should be you that the twins decide to befriend?' he asked.

A certain—suspicious?—nuance in his voice had her returning his look indignantly. 'Well, it wasn't because I

fished for a guided tour of my own, if that's what you're
thinking!' she retorted. 'I only met them by chance
because they almost fell over me on the beach and when
they stopped to apologise we got talking. As to why they
offered to show me some of Hermitage . . .' her mouth
tilted ruefully, 'I think that was because they felt I
might have been lonely since I was on my own.'

'Matthew only having arranged fishing trips for himself, of course,' Steele charged drily.

'He—he doesn't consider fishing a suitable sport for
women. At least, not for me, he doesn't,' she attempted to
explain with a shaky laugh, and promptly sought to
direct the conversation into less personal channels.
'What a beautiful place this is,' she sighed as the track
led them beneath the cover of thickly clustered trees.
'Have you owned it for long?'

'Nearly three years,' he told her offhandedly. 'It had
been allowed to become very run-down, but Vance and
Erin thought it had possibilities, so we bought it. They're
gradually getting it how they want it, though, and once
the heli-pad goes in next year they'll be able to offer
accommodation for all ages.'

'And the name, Morning Retreat,' she pondered. 'Did
you call it that?'

'No, that's the one it came with,' he advised with a
rueful shaping of his lips and a shake of his head. 'Although it's not quite the original.'

'Oh?' She eyed him curiously.

'Mmm, initially it was Mourning—with a u—Retreat,
but when the islands were first converted into a holiday
resort, someone apparently didn't consider it a very
appropriate name and decided to delete that particular
letter from the spelling,' he disclosed wryly.

Ravelle could understand why. 'It sounds as if there
may be a history attached to the place,' she half smiled.

'I guess you could say that,' he allowed, but on a

slightly roughening note. 'Some feller wanted to cut himself off from the world last century when his wife deserted him for someone else, so he came out here to mourn her loss for close on twenty years.' He uttered a short, mocking laugh. 'It seems men are never going to learn that women are only faithful for as long as it suits them, doesn't it?'

'Men being models of fidelity, I suppose?' she gibed immediately. In view of his past behaviour, she hardly thought he was in a position to criticise.

'I'm not about to break *my* engagement, honey.'

The unfairness of the retort had her temperature rising rapidly. 'It's only at your insistence that I am!' she flared. 'Besides, from what I hear, you didn't have any qualms about disposing of *your* fiancée when it was convenient to you!'

'Except that happened to be by mutual consent,' he relayed complacently.

'Meaning, she accepted the money offered?'

As soon as the recklessly goading accusation left her lips Ravelle wished she could recall it. Not because it was a charge she regretted—after all, Steele deserved all the denunciation she could heap on him in her estimation—but because she regretted raking up the past so explicitly. With her parents' help she had lived through the agony of his callous rejection, but face to face with him she very much doubted she could hide the pain that spurning had engendered.

In the meantime, Steele's mouth had levelled ominously, his eyes taking on a flinty hue. 'Fortunately, there was no need to make an offer. Kathleen was a completely different type from you!' he retaliated in savagely biting tones.

For a fraction of a second Ravelle stared at him wordlessly, then with tears welling into her eyes and her teeth catching at her bottom lip to stop its trembling, she turned her head away to stare hazily at the trees beside the path.

'Yes, well, I g-guess you can be lucky s-sometimes, can't you?' she half laughed, half choked, in an effort to disguise how degraded he'd made her feel. 'And—and just to prove it,' she continued in the same unsteadily flippant voice on hearing the moke approaching on its return journey, 'you'll no doubt be r-relieved to hear I've changed m-my mind about seeing Hermitage t-today. I think I'll go back to Hideaway with the t-twins instead.'

Craig and Dion must have mistaken her promptly waved signal as one urging them to hurry, however, for there was no sign of them slowing down as they passed with the cry, 'We'll be back soon,' left floating on the dusty air behind them.

Tears of frustration coupled with those of anguish, and with her face still averted Ravelle spun around, intending to follow them.

'Now where do you think you're going, for crying out loud?' demanded Steele in a less than patient tone.

'I told you . . . t-to the r-resort,' she stammered huskily, heading away from him. 'I'll wait on the beach till the tide goes out and then walk across.'

'Stop being so damned childish!' She wasn't even aware he'd taken the steps necessary to catch her until a forceful hand on her arm pulled her around to face him— a hand which then proceeded to tilt her face inexorably up to his. 'Oh, hell, don't tell me you're crying again!' he groaned in rueful irritation on seeing the unmistakable dampness spreading from her long lashes to her cheeks.

'Of course I'm not,' she protested, even as she wiped the tips of shaking fingers across her eyes. 'I got some dust in my eye, that's all.'

'Both of them?'

'Yes!'

'And your voice always quavers when that happens, does it?'

Ravelle held his taunting gaze helplessly. She was fooling no one but herself, and the realisation had her shoulders drooping in defeat. 'Okay, so I was crying,' she finally admitted dismally. 'But then that was your intention, wasn't it? In revenge for my having had the temerity to—to . . .'

'Make a crack that was best left unsaid?' Steele stroked a finger absently along the vulnerable line of her jaw. 'If you don't like the shooting, honey, you shouldn't declare war.'

And especially not against a marksman of his calibre, she brooded silently, forlornly. Whether she had right on her side or not didn't seem to count. He had that streak of implacability in him which would always give him the advantage.

'In fact,' he started speaking again, his lips quirking ironically, 'since we share a daughter whom I plan on seeing for the first time in the very near future, perhaps it would be more reasonable—if only for her sake—if we practised putting our differences aside so that we can show, if not an enamoured front, then at least a cordial one in her presence. I hardly think warring parents are likely to appeal to any child, and certainly not to one who's never known a father before.'

Disturbingly aware of his touch as his trailing finger came to rest beneath her chin, Ravelle swallowed and attempted a weak half smile of acquiescence. 'I—I suppose you're right,' she had no option but to concede. The effect their possible sniping might have on Samara had been worrying her too. 'It's going to be hard enough trying to explain everything to her as it is. It would be so much more simple if she could just remain Samara Fenton, you know.'

'Thereby relegating me to an interested, but unrelated,

visitor? Uh-uh, no deal!' Steele vetoed decisively. 'The
time's more than due for her not only to know that she
has a father, but that she's also entitled—among other
things—to his name.'

Ravelle grimaced wryly. 'At her age I somehow doubt
if that consideration is likely to mean much to her.'

'Maybe not, but it does to me,' came the prompt
return. 'And since I presume from our conversation last
night that it's myself you've registered as her father, then
I fail to see why you should consider explaining the
change in name is going to be so difficult.'

'Because she thinks her father's dead! My fictitious
husband, remember?' she part groaned, part wailed.

'Sorry to be so unobliging,' he drawled facetiously, and
plainly referring to her first comment. 'But if it's my
name on the birth certificate, perhaps you wouldn't mind
telling me just how you intended to explain the discrepancy between that name and your supposed
husband's when the time came?' His eyes suddenly
narrowed astutely. 'Or did his name just happen to be
Cunningham too, by any chance?'

'It—er—seemed the most logical choice under the
circumstances,' she owned uncomfortably, moving restlessly under his intent gaze. 'I couldn't bring myself to
leave a blank on the registration form where her father's
name was supposed to go, or—or to completely fabricate
one—it was just too important—so it followed . . .'

'That I should suffer an early demise in order to keep
the records straight, is that it?'

There was nothing in either his expression or his voice
to give her a clue as to what he might have been thinking,
and she began chewing at her lip nervously. 'I'm sorry,
but it appeared the right solution at the time, and—
and . . .,' she blinked furiously as a treacherous moisture
started to mist her vision, 'I certainly didn't expect ever
to see you again.'

'Yes, well, I guess . . .' He stopped, peering at her closely, and then with a disbelieving shake of his head, a rueful smile edged across his mouth as he lightly touched a finger to her dewy lashes. 'Not more tears?' he quizzed on a teasing note. 'I grant you, your story may have created problems, but they're not unsolvable, you know.'

Thankful he believed that had been the cause of her momentary loss of control, Ravelle was all too anxious not to disabuse him of the misconception and hunched one smoothly tanned shoulder negligently. 'No, I suppose not.'

With an encouraging smile which immediately sent her emotions reeling capriciously once more, Steele laid an arm casually around her back and, gathering his patiently waiting mount's reins in his other hand, recommenced guiding her down the track.

'Nonetheless, I rather think you're hoping for miracles in respect to Inglis,' he speculated drily as they walked.

Two deep creases made their appearance between winging brows. 'What makes you say that?'

'Well, don't you reckon he'll consider it one hell of a coincidence that your husband's name and mine happen to be the same?' he countered in wry amusement. 'I mean, just how many Steele Cunninghams do you think one person's likely to meet in the space of four years?'

'Oh, but I never referred to you by your first name. I— I thought that might have been too distinctive,' she confessed a trifle selfconsciously. 'When I couldn't avoid giving my husband's name I used to say it was Pat. You know, from your second name, Patterson? Besides, I don't think Matthew even knows what my husband's name was supposed to be, otherwise I'm pretty sure he would have put two and two together by now,' Her eyes widened eloquently.

Steele's expression was one of amazement. 'You've got to be kidding!' he half laughed incredulously.

'About what?'

'That he doesn't know your husband's name.' Now it was his turn to frown, although his demeanour still held a certain amount of disbelief. 'You're not honestly trying to tell me he's never been interested enough to enquire at least that much about the person he intended marrying, are you?'

'I—well—I went to Sydney to have Samara, and that's where my husband was supposed to have lived. Matthew doesn't know anyone there, so I guess he figured it wouldn't mean anything to him even if he had asked,' she relayed with a shrug.

'Didn't his indifference disappoint you?'

'Disappoint me?' she repeated sardonically. 'I was relieved! After all, the facts surrounding my—er—marriage weren't exactly capable of withstanding an in-depth investigation.'

'Even so, I'd have thought he'd display just a little curiosity about your life before you met him.' Abruptly he grinned and, caught unprepared, Ravelle felt her heart lurch painfully. 'He certainly seemed to yesterday afternoon when he discovered that wasn't our first meeting.'

'That was—was different,' she defended loyally, if a little breathlessly. That easy smile of his had always had the power to make her pulse quicken. 'You purposely set out to make him believe there'd been something between us.'

'And there hadn't been?' One dark brow tilted whimsically.

With Samara the result, she was hardly in a position to deny it, but that didn't stop her giving him an extremely expressive look in return. 'There wasn't any need for you to as good as tell him so, though, was there?' she retorted. Then, sighing, 'Although I suppose it won't be long before just about everyone knows. What did Erin and

Vance say when you told them you had a daughter?'

Steele expelled a long breath, his eyes crinkling at the corners as he appeared to scan the horizon. 'I didn't tell them,' was his heavily voiced divulgence.

'I see,' tautly.

'Meaning?'

'Oh, nothing.'

'Ravelle!' The hand which had been around her back now slipped upwards to grasp the nape of her neck, impelling her to face him. *'Meaning?'* he reiterated relentlessly.

She hunched both shoulders in a gesture of feigned unconcern. 'Only that I understand your position. It was a—a stupid question to ask.'

'Then maybe you'd also care to enlighten me as to why.'

'Well, naturally you wouldn't tell them, would you?' she made herself smile lightly. 'I mean, you'd hardly want your family to know you had an illegitimate child, let alone that someone of *my* type was its mother.'

The grip on her neck tightened hurtfully. 'Then in that case, perhaps you can also explain why I'm insisting that that same illegitimate child carries *my* name, and why I originally intended taking her home with me, if I didn't want my family to know about her. Or did you think I'd planned to tell them I'd found her . . . in the nearest cabbage patch?' he stabbed at her irately, and shaking her so hard she wondered her teeth didn't rattle.

Temporarily she had forgotten his earlier intentions, but even now that he had reminded her, she was still wary. 'Well, why didn't you tell them, then?' she demanded suspiciously.

'Because I thought it would be easier on *you* if I didn't, that's why!'

'Oh!' Feeling foolish at having misjudged his reasons so completely, yet at the same time inordinately pleased that his decision had been made out of deference to herself, Ravelle glanced embarrassedly upwards from the cover of long dark lashes. 'Then thank you,' she murmured shyly. 'I would prefer it if no one else knew until—until after I've broken my engagement to Matthew.'

'You haven't said anything to him yet, presumably?' on a still rough note.

'I haven't really had a chance. I wasn't exactly in the mood for it last night, and I didn't see him before he left this morning. Actually, that's what I was doing when the twins stumbled over me. Working out the best way in which to tell him.'

'The result of which was . . .?'

'Nothing very inspiring, I'm afraid,' she confessed ruefully.

Releasing his hold on her, Steele dropped his hand on to his hip, his expression losing none of its previous exasperation. 'I wouldn't have thought that much inspiration was really necessary! Why can't you just tell him it's over between you, and be done with it? It's not as if you have to worry about whether you should return his ring or not. The man apparently didn't even see fit to give you one!' A certain gibing contempt crept into his voice as he eyed her left hand sardonically.

Ravelle immediately began fiddling with the wedding ring she did have on her finger. 'No, well, he—we—decided it was a luxury we could do without,' she offered selfconsciously. 'But what I'm worried about is that if I don't watch what I say, Matthew's likely to become . . .'

'Violent?'

'*Suspicious*,' she contradicted resolutely. 'Anyway, I think it would be extremely unfair if I more or less just walked out on him as you suggest.'

His lip curled cynically. 'I don't seem to remember you being that considerate four years ago!'

'Would you wonder?' indignation had her flashing back immediately. 'Your parting gesture was hardly designed to give my spirits a lift, was it?'

'Oh, I don't know,' he shrugged reflectively. 'I would have thought so . . . considering.'

Considering he hadn't been obliged to offer her anything, she supposed bitterly, a lump of despair settling in her throat and stopping her from speaking, although not from condemning him with desolate and reproachful eyes.

'Okay, I'm sorry!' he apologised abruptly in a harsh tone, rubbing a hand irritably around his neck.

Ravelle's glance became guardedly questioning. Could he possibly mean for that cheque?

'For also letting loose with a gibe that was best left unsaid,' Steele responded to her unspoken query with a sigh. 'I guess it's your prerogative to deal with Inglis however you wish, and has nothing whatsoever to do with the manner in which we parted.'

Cloaking her disappointment with the thought that at least he had apologised for his taunt, she put out a tentative hand to touch his arm, then swiftly withdrew it. 'Well, the circumstances are different,' she offered in a conciliatory fashion.

Surprisingly, some of the tenseness left his features and his mouth shaped wryly. 'With someone of Inglis's frigid disposition, that was a foregone conclusion,' he drawled.

Ravelle's cheeks burnt with the heat of embarrassment. 'Those weren't the circumstances I was talking about!'

'Perhaps not, although that still doesn't alter the facts. He treats you like an emotionless possession, honey.'

At least that was better than having one's feelings abused! 'Maybe I prefer it that way,' she smiled bittersweetly.

His half smile widened to a distinct grin. 'After your

response to being kissed last night, I'm sure you'll pardon me if I say, and maybe pigs can fly too,' he mocked.

To her chagrin Ravelle flushed again, guiltily. There was little she could say in her own defence and, rather than attempt to, she pretended to ignore his goading remark. Unfortunately, though, it did tend to summon recollections which were a great deal more difficult to disregard, and the more so as the day progressed, she was to discover to her dismay.

CHAPTER SEVEN

As THE sleek lines of the cabin cruiser became visible on the horizon, Ravelle sank down on to the edge of the jetty where it met the beach, and with her bare feet digging pleasurably into the warm sand, prepared to wait for Matthew's return from his fishing trip. Her thoughts drifted musingly, and in no way connected with the boat's arrival, but solely concentrating on her own experiences of the day.

It had been fascinating having three such competent guides showing her over Hermitage, and with Steele being as amiably indulgent as she had ever known him to be once the twins rejoined them, there had been absolutely nothing to mar her enjoyment. By the time they returned to the resort in the late afternoon she doubted if there was anything of interest she hadn't seen, and she was thoroughly in agreement with Dion and Craig's opinion that Mariner Bay was just about the best beach on either island.

Of course, the idea did intrude occasionally that it might have been Steele's compliant presence which had made everything seem so wonderfully satisfying—he had

always had the power to make her feel excitingly alive—
but with a dismissing shake of her head she refused to
allow her thoughts to dwell on that aspect any longer
than they did on any other.

After lunch they had all donned the masks, snorkels
and flippers the twins had carried back with them, along
with a hamper of delicious food, and gone diving beneath
the warm clear waters of the lagoon to see the marine life
at close hand. It was incredible to Ravelle that the
brilliantly hued fish should accept their presence so
unworriedly, but it appeared that as long as they made
no sudden movements to scare them, the sea-dwellers
were quite prepared to welcome newcomers to their
beautiful underwater habitat.

Later, as the tide receded, Dion and Craig had been
only too pleased to explain the mysteries of the exposed
reef to her, and although she had been somewhat wary at
first on hearing the coral crack beneath her sneakered
feet—Erin had sent a pair over since it was impossible to
walk on the reef without suitable protection because of
its sharpness—it didn't take long for her to forget all
about the noise as her whole attention became riveted by
the amazingly varied life-forms laid bare by the ebbing
sea.

Naturally enough, the greatest part of the reef con-
sisted of hard corals—staghorn, mushroom, brain—the
softer species scattered freely among them, but not
nearly so attractive now that their colonies of connecting
polyps had emptied of water as they had been when
viewed from under the water. Embedded in the rubble
between, large clams displayed velvety-looking mantles
in the richest colour combinations of emerald and purple,
orange and peacock, while pale green algae like tiny
grapes shared coral pools with swaying sea grass and
vivid blue, red, and orange sea stars.

They had stayed on the reef inspecting all manner of

associated creatures until the tide turned, and now, as
Ravelle sat waiting for the cruiser to negotiate the narrow
navigation channel, the whole of the reef and the sand-
spit between the two islands had disappeared once more
from view.

The powerful throb of the boat's engines quietened to
a muted hum as it approached the jetty and, brushing
the sand from the back of her shorts, Ravelle made her
way towards it. Matthew, she noted, was the first person
ashore, before the tying up had even been completed.

'How did it go? Did you catch anything?' she asked
interestedly on reaching him.

'Catch anything!' he echoed with a disgusted snort. 'I
never even got a line wet!'

'Oh, what a pity,' she commiserated sympathetically.
'Weren't they biting today?'

'How should I know?' he snapped irritably, and running his fingers over what she could now see was a
decidedly pale forehead. 'I was too damned sick to leave
my bunk all day. There's a mountainous swell out there,
and that unseaworthy tub,' with an outflung hand to
indicate the gleaming-hulled cruiser, 'just wasn't capable
of handling the conditions. Or maybe it was the captain
who was the unqualified one!' He cast a malevolent
glance to where Vance still stood at the helm.

Since his disparaging remark had been made in tones
loud enough to carry, Ravelle directed an embarrassed
smile of apology towards the man in the boat and
received a wry grin in response. It was apparent none of
the other members of the excursion party had similar
ideas, though, she noticed, for they all appeared very
satisfied, and appreciative, as they called out their fare-
wells before leaving. Nor did any of them seem to have
suffered from Matthew's malaise either, she realised
ruefully.

'I should think Vance would have to have a licence, or

a ticket, or whatever they call it, before taking members of the public out to sea,' she proposed contemplatively as they began making for the path. 'Otherwise they'd be leaving themselves open to all sorts of claims if something untoward occurred.' Her lips curved with dry humour. 'And somehow I just can't see the Cunninghams being that amateurish.'

'In other words, they're automatically right and I'm wrong—again—is that it?'

Sighing, she spread her hands helplessly. 'Well, I'd hardly call that,' nodding over her shoulder to indicate the superb craft he'd just left, 'an unseaworthy tub, and it does seem as if—as if everyone else enjoyed the trip.'

'So?' Matthew stared at her stonily.

'So I think you may have inadvertently allowed your—er—indisposition to have distorted your judgment a little.'

'Oh, do you? Do you really?' he sneered sarcastically. 'Well, thank you for your loyalty! I should have known it was too much to expect you to see my point of view for a change. You've done nothing else but fall all over yourself in your anxiety to fawn on the Cunninghams ever since we arrived. Anyone would think you were a part of the family, the way you jump to their defence every time.'

Ravelle's eyes widened sardonically. 'Because I said you seemed to be the only one with any complaints about the trip?'

'Because you couldn't wait to imply that I had to be the one in the wrong!'

'Well, maybe I just happen to think you are,' she burst out, her own temper flaring. 'I don't necessarily have to agree with every opinion of yours, you know, Matthew!'

'And definitely not when the Cunninghams are involved, eh?'

'You don't leave me much choice, since you appear determined to find fault with everything they do. I'm only trying to be fair.'

'To whom?' he gibed scornfully.

'To whoever I consider is in the right,' she retorted with some asperity, then gave a weary shake of her head as she sent him a speculative sideways look. 'Goodness only knows why, but you've changed since we've been here, Matthew. You're not the same person any more.'

Hazel eyes returned her gaze truculently. 'While you are, I suppose?' he retaliated in rancorous tones. 'Why, ever since I came back to find you in the dining room with the arrogant bastard Steele Cunningham, you've done nothing but criticise my every move! No, *you're* the one who's altered, Ravelle, and not for the better, I might add. Your behaviour has been most disappointing, not to mention selfish, from the moment we arrived.'

While his had been exemplary, she presumed irefully. 'Then in order to eliminate any chance of me disillusioning you further, perhaps it would be best if we broke our engagement here and now!' she flashed on the spur of the moment.

'So you can feel free to chase after Cunningham unhindered?' he insinuated savagely.

'No!' she denied, aghast. The last thing she wanted was for him to think Steele had anything to do with her suggestion. 'I told you before, he means nothing to me!' Well, she shrugged inwardly, dispiritedly, she certainly meant nothing to him, and that made the result the same.

Matthew stepped from the jetty on to the sand, his expression one of self-satisfaction now. 'That being so, then I can see no call for us to break our engagement,' he relayed autocratically.

'Except that we seem to do nothing but quarrel these days,' she just had to remind him tartly.

'*You* quarrel, Ravelle,' he contradicted peremptorily. 'And usually at the most inopportune times. I would have thought you'd have a little more compassion than to be picking arguments after all I've been through today. You know, it took me quite a while yesterday just to recover from the trip out here.'

With a resigned shrug for her lost opportunity she apologised cursorily. 'I'm sorry.' Then, feeling she should make some offer, 'Is there anything you'd like me to get for you?'

Almost to his cabin now, he sighed dramatically. 'No, I don't think so. Peace and quiet are what I need at the moment.' Putting a foot on to the first step, he halted and turned. 'Oh, you'd better arrange to have your dinner in your own unit tonight. I'm sure I won't be able to stand the smell of food, much less eat any before tomorrow. Perhaps if you come round after breakfast I'll have recovered sufficiently to spend some time with you.'

'I'll look forward to it,' Ravelle averred, lips twitching wryly. He hadn't worried about spending any time with her when his fishing trip had been in the offing. 'About ten, will that be okay?'

A few minutes later, after having received his confirmation and wished him a speedy recuperation, Ravelle set off in the direction of the reception building in order to advise Erin that Matthew wouldn't be requiring a meal that evening. She found the friendly redhead sorting out accounts at the desk while at the same time engaging in a desultory conversation with her sister who was lazing elegantly in a cane chair opposite.

'Oh, hi!' Erin smiled on looking up to see who had entered. 'How did you enjoy your day on Hermitage? The twins were tickled pink with the idea of being your *official*,' with laughing emphasis, 'guides, and they've talked of nothing else ever since they returned.'

'They were certainly extremely conscientious ones. I

think we must have scoured every inch of that island before they were satisfied I'd seen all there was to see,' Ravelle disclosed with an answering grin. 'And thank you for going to so much trouble with the lunch you sent over with them. It was really nice.'

'Oh, you don't have to thank me,' came the quick disclaimer. 'That's what we're here for, to make your stay as pleasant as possible.'

'Although it isn't customary for you to provide picnic lunches, is it, Erin?' inserted her sister, pointedly enquiring. 'I mean to say, the whole resort's not so large that people can't make it back to the restaurant, no matter where they happen to be, surely?'

Ravelle's face tightened at the implied rebuke, but it was Erin who spoke first. 'Mmm, normally they do,' she shrugged, making light of it. 'But it's not an unusual request for the twins, so it hardly created any extra work in expanding the amount to suit four instead of two.'

'Ah, yes, I heard Steele had been persuaded to join the party.' Pale green eyes swept over Ravelle hostilely, then switched to the older woman behind the desk. 'I thought he said he had a lot to do today and that's why he wouldn't be coming over here until later,' Chantal recalled on a near-accusing note.

Erin merely hunched her shoulders to indicate her ignorance of the reason, then, surprisingly, aimed a vaguely humorous look of enquiry at Ravelle which was initially answered with a rueful shake of her blonde head.

'I wouldn't know about that,' she followed up with a half smile, half grimace. 'Maybe he finished earlier than expected. We just happened to meet when the twins were on their way to collect the fruit you wanted, and he *offered*,' for Chantal's benefit, 'to accompany us.'

'That was convenient!' the other girl immediately sniped.

'For him, or us?' quizzed Ravelle sweetly, and just as

promptly. She was getting a little tired of Chantal's innuendoes. Unaccountably, the coy femme fatale of yesterday evening was all claws today.

Chantal's lips thinned ominously, but before she could give vent to her rancour Erin swiftly pre-empted her by asking, 'And—er—how did Matthew like his day of reef fishing? I haven't seen Vance since his return to find out how it went, but there were certainly some good sized fish taken into the kitchen a while back, so I presume it was a success in that regard.'

'Yes, well, apparently not for Matthew by all accounts,' Ravelle supplied awkwardly. 'Unfortunately, he didn't travel particularly well and, as a consequence, wasn't able to even try his hand at the fishing.'

Behind her Chantal made a spluttering sound midway between choked laughter and a snort of disbelief, but which she determinedly ignored. On the other hand, Erin's expression changed to one of obvious dismay.

'Oh, what a shame!' she exclaimed. 'He appeared so keen to go too.'

'Mmm, but I believe there was quite a swell running and, I'm afraid, that's what put paid to his participation.'

'A swell? Today?' Chantal challenged contemptuously. 'It was as calm as a millpond!'

In all honesty Ravelle couldn't refute the assertion. In her estimation too the sea had looked remarkably peaceful, but for Matthew's sake she half smiled diffidently and speculated, 'Perhaps it was rougher on the outer reef.'

The downward turn of the other girl's mouth expressed her opinion of that supposition with crystal clarity, but Erin was prepared to be a little more charitable.

'It could have been, I guess,' she granted. 'But I expect he's recovered by now anyway, hasn't he?'

'Actually, no, I'm sorry to say he hasn't yet,' Ravelle reluctantly had to inform her. 'That's the reason for my being here . . . to let you know Matthew would rather not have a meal this evening. It—er—always takes him a time to get over any form of illness.'

'Apparently he has what he calls a *delicate* constitution,' Chantal stressed derisively for her sister's further edification.

'Oh?' Erin's brows peaked expressively. 'That must be very frustrating for him.'

Personally, Ravelle thought he found the idea of being confined to bed rather more satisfying than frustrating, but not for one moment would she be so disloyal as to say so. Instead she half smiled as if in agreement and bantered, 'It certainly was today, that's for sure!'

'Then, if that means you'll be on your own tonight, you'll join us for dinner again, of course.' Erin made her invitation sound more like a foregone conclusion, but Ravelle shook her head hastily.

'No really, that's very nice of you, but I don't want to impose. For one thing, it makes your numbers uneven,' she joked lightly, 'and for another, I was only intending to have a light meal in my unit and then write some letters home.'

Besides, she added whimsically to herself, with Chantal in such a malicious mood it didn't exactly presage a pleasant evening, and nor did she think it advisable to be in Steele's company too often. To put herself in the position where she could be burnt twice by the same flame would be the height of stupidity, not to mention catastrophic to her emotions.

'Oh, but you've plenty of time to write your letters. The boat doesn't arrive again for another two days,' Erin advised. 'And what does it matter if our numbers are odd? I'm positive you couldn't prefer to eat on your own. No, I won't hear of it,' she smiled engagingly, but decisively for all that. 'You're having dinner with us, and that's all there is to it.'

In the face of such insistence there seemed very little

Ravelle could do but accede, and she did so with wry resignation.

As she had suspected, however, the evening proved to be a not particularly relaxing one as far as Ravelle was concerned. Not only was she continually, perturbingly, aware of Steele's overwhelming presence on her right—albeit due to entirely different reasons than those which had produced her unease of the night before—but Chantal showed no inclination to disguise her recent upsurge of antagonism, leaving no doubt in Ravelle's mind, at least, that the pale-eyed girl definitely hadn't been in accord with her sister's invitation for Ravelle to join them.

Eventually, the strain involved in attempting to dismiss one from her thoughts and parry the other's increasingly unsubtle sarcasms became just too much of an effort and, when she judged a suitable time had elapsed after their meal had been concluded, Ravelle took her leave politely—if a little stiltedly—and set off across the patio in the direction of her unit with a heaved sigh of relief.

Only to find on reaching the appropriate path that Chantal—ostensibly on her way to the powder room—was determinedly trailing her. In a lavender-coloured Gucci-designed gown, the older girl looked every inch the wealthy, self-assured socialite as she came to a swirling halt, her head angled superciliously aloft, before Ravelle's resignedly waiting figure. There had seemed little point in trying to avoid her if she was this intent on having something to say.

'You're wasting your time, you know,' she began with a decided smirk.

'In hoping to sleep while the muttonbirds are still making a noise?' Ravelle queried flippantly, brows lifting. They had a disconcerting habit of sounding like a

young baby crying, although she guessed that it hadn't
been her welfare which had prompted Chantal to make
the remark.

'I meant, your transparent infatuation with Steele!'
was the jeering retort. 'Not content with using Dion and
Craig as a means of claiming his attention today, you
then have the presumption to share our table for dinner
in an attempt to continue doing the same all evening!
Except that it wasn't successful, was it? You could have
been a piece of the furniture for all the interest Steele
showed in you,' she laughed mockingly. 'So little, in fact,
that I wasn't surprised you finally decided to leave. I
suppose in the end you must have realised all your efforts
were in vain.'

'Then why bother to deliver the surely unnecessary
warning that I'm wasting my time?' Ravelle quizzed
wryly, hiding her dismay behind a shell of feigned
amusement. Steele had been somewhat preoccupied,
that was true, but more importantly, and disastrously,
she feared Chantal's obvious exaggeration with regard to
herself could unwittingly have predicted the future. If
she wasn't careful, she could very well find herself in
danger of falling for Steele all over again!

'Because I feel sorry for you, naturally!' Chantal
answered her question in tones filled with patronising
hauteur. 'Since you have nothing more exciting to look
forward to than a lifetime spent with that self-centred,
pompous ass of a fiancé, I can understand how someone
with Steele's air of undeniable masculinity would appeal
to you. But I can assure you, you're not the first female
by any means to give him the come-on, it happens all
the time, and although he may indulge in an occasional
affair, they never last for long, and you can be certain
he'll never make any permanent commitment to someone
of . . .' her darkened eyebrows arched sardonically,
'shall we say, your insignificant social standing?'

A fact she knew only too well, reflected Ravelle disconsolately, but it did serve as a timely reminder and her chin lifted challengingly. 'Yours either, apparently, since he's already broken one engagement to someone who was, I gather, eminently suitable,' she pointed out dulcetly.

'Huh, Kathleen! She was a fool!' Chantal denigrated scornfully. 'She had absolutely no conception how to manage a man of Steele's rugged individualism.'

'Whereas you do!'

'Oh, yes,' Chantal averred with insufferable smugness. 'I know exactly how to handle Steele Cunningham, believe me.'

'By being satisfied to fill in between his occasional affairs?' Ravelle couldn't resist gibing. The desire to prick the other girl's inflated ego was almost overwhelming.

Chantal's face erupted into brilliant colour, her skin a vivid scarlet, her eyes a vitriolic green. Then, with what was obviously a superhuman effort, she smiled tightly, tauntingly.

'Even if that were true, I've no doubt you'd still jump at the chance to change places with me. As I'm sure we both know, to fill in for some men is far more rewarding than to a constant companion for others.' Her mouth curled into a contemptuous sneer. 'Especially if they happen to be pitiful specimens of manhood like Matthew!'

It was the second time she had spoken in such derogatory terms about her fiancé, but Ravelle didn't mean to let it pass again. 'You didn't appear to think that way yesterday evening, I noticed . . . while you were throwing yourself at him!' she recalled sarcastically.

'Throwing myself at *him*? Darling, I'd as soon throw myself on to a bed of nails as I would at Matthew!' Chantal declared theatrically, simpering. Oh, what a joke! I wouldn't have believed it possible that even the most besotted of fiancées could imagine for one moment that *I* would find him interesting.' She laughed spitefully. 'I was amusing myself, that's all. He takes himself so seriously that I thought it would be fun to lead him on a little before bringing him down to earth by letting him know just what an excruciating bore he really is.'

So that was what had been behind her unexpected behaviour of the previous night! Ravelle's sympathies were all with Matthew. Granted, he might not have possessed the most endearing disposition in the world, but after such a cold-blooded revelation she hardly thought that Chantal's was any more likeable.

'Then all I can say is, you have a very sick sense of humour, and I hope Matthew retaliated with a few home truths for your education when you made your nauseating disclosure!' she denounced witheringly.

'Oh, but I haven't told him yet,' Chantal smiled, unperturbed. 'I was planning to wait until we'd had that game of table tennis I promised him. From what I saw, he's nowhere near as good as he likes to think he is, and I thought it would be rather appropriate to beat him hollow at that and *then* deliver my *coup de grâce*!' Her demeanour was one of supreme self-confidence. 'As I hinted yesterday—only Matthew was too wrapped up in himself to take heed—I am a first-rate player.'

'As well as a first-rate bitch, apparently!' Ravelle couldn't contain her mounting disgust any longer.

'Don't you dare call *me* names, you scheming, two-faced slut! You've pushed yourself in where you're not wanted once too often, so let that . . .' Chantal whipped her open hand forcefully across Ravelle's cheek, 'be a lesson to you! Keep your amorous glances for Matthew from now on, or you'll find there's worse to come!' she hissed.

'*Chantal!*' From out of the darkness Erin's voice called

in dismayed censure before Ravelle had a chance to recover from the unexpected physical attack. 'What in blazes do you think you're doing?' her sister demanded furiously on reaching them.

'Issuing a warning!' Chantal spat, not the slightest chastised. 'I'm not having her calling me names, or creeping around Steele at every opportunity, and the sooner she realises it the better off she'll be. If she's dissatisfied with her fiancé that's her bad luck, but she's not going to attach herself to mine!'

'Steele isn't your fiancé,' Erin disputed, tight-lipped.

'Not at the moment, perhaps, but he soon will be!'

'Well, whether he will or not, I still refuse to condone your action in treating one of our guests in such a manner, and I suggest you apologise . . . immediately!'

'To her?' Chantal queried disdainfully, and not a little horrified. 'I'm damned if I will! She asked for it, and in any case, the pair of them—she and her whining fiancé—have done nothing but upset everyone since they set foot on the island. Personally, I'm of the opinion they should be the ones to apologise—and then be told to leave, so that the rest of us can go back to enjoying ourselves!'

Erin's sharp intake of breath was an angry one. 'Then perhaps I should remind you that Ravelle and Matthew are paying guests here—you're not!—so if anyone is requested to leave the island it will more than likely be you!'

'You mean you'd make your own sister leave, rather than them?' in patent disbelief.

'If I have to . . . yes!' Erin's reply came unwaveringly. 'Vance and I have gone to a lot of trouble to ensure that Hideaway has a good reputation, and I don't intend to see it jeopardised by any hot-tempered action of yours. So, under the circumstances, I think an apology is the least you can offer.'

'Oh, please, Erin, there's no need,' Ravelle cut in hurriedly, not wanting to be the cause of dissension between the two sisters. 'I'm as much to blame as Chantal is. It was a—a personal misunderstanding, that's all. Certainly not a reflection on Vance's and your management.'

'Like hell it was a misunderstanding!' Chantal gritted. 'And I don't need you doing me any favours either! I have no intention of apologising, whether you want one or not, and if that makes me unwelcome on this island, then so be it! I'd rather leave than say I'm sorry to you!' she sneered as she whirled around, skirts billowing, to storm off in the direction of the beer garden.

With a regretful curve to her lips Erin looked across at the younger girl. 'Well, if Chantal won't apologise, I will, on her behalf,' she declared.

'I'd rather you didn't,' Ravelle instantly demurred, shaking her head. 'It certainly wasn't your fault and if—if Chantal and Steele are . . .'

'But that's just it, as far as I'm aware they're not,' interrupted Erin. 'Oh, he may be a regular escort when he's in town, and to my knowledge there isn't any other female in his life at present, but as to them being on the verge of becoming engaged . . .' She shrugged, explicitly, and didn't bother finishing, but mused instead, 'Besides, I don't think they're particularly suited.'

As much as Ravelle would have loved to ask the reasoning behind the comment, she didn't think she could appear detached enough to do so with equanimity, and so merely hunched one shoulder, saying nothing.

'Nevertheless, I can understand to some extent why Chantal might feel threatened by your presence,' Erin continued wryly, but in the same contemplative fashion.

'You also think I—I'm trying to a-attract Steele?' Ravelle stammered, appalled, and completely unprepared.

'Well, I don't know I'd go so far as to say that, but . . .' Erin paused expressively, 'there's certainly an unmistakable feeling of tension in the air whenever you're together.'

'I told you we didn't exactly part the best of friends,' Ravelle evaded, hopefully nonchalant.

'Hmm, and is that also why he watches you like a hawk the whole time . . . four years later?'

'I d-didn't know he did.'

'You surprise me,' quipped Erin drily. 'The more so since I've noticed your eyes—surreptitiously, I admit— very rarely stray from him for long either.'

Ravelle forced a light, amazed laugh past the knot in her throat. 'I hadn't realised that—and if it's true, then I can assure you it's quite unintentional.'

'Oh, it's true all right,' Erin half laughed whimsically, but on seeing Ravelle's nervously worried expression, she sobered and laid a hand gently on her arm. 'I'm sorry, I guess you must think Chantal and I are two of a kind, with all our insinuations. If you told me to shut up and mind my own business I wouldn't blame you in the slightest.'

'No, you've been too understanding with all the problems Matthew and I have, one way or another, presented you with for me to do that,' Ravelle declared softly, sincerely.

'But you wish to hell I'd give it a rest all the same.'

Undecided as to just how she should reply without either giving offence or lying, Erin suddenly relieved her of the necessity by laughing wryly, 'Okay, I get the message. I'll let you get the early night you wanted and we'll see you in the morning, hmm?'

Ravelle nodded gratefully, and as soon as Erin had made her departure continued on to her cabin deep in thought—the same thoughts which kept her awake long after she had reached her bed. She was becoming all too aware just why her eyes continually strayed in Steele's

direction, but why—if what Erin intimated was correct—
should he be watching her so intently in turn? That she
just couldn't fathom.

CHAPTER EIGHT

'You're being ridiculous! She was joking with you, and
you've obviously taken it the wrong way,' declared
Matthew in his most superior manner.

On visiting his cabin the following morning Ravelle
had found him—somewhat to her surprise—fully
recovered from the effects of his inauspicious fishing trip.
From previous experience she had quite expected him to
take at least twenty-four hours before admitting to
complete recuperation.

On hearing his stated intention to seek out Chantal
in order to claim the table tennis match she had promised
him, however, Ravelle had first sought to discourage him
by suggesting a game of mini-golf instead. When this
had proved unsuccessful she'd had no choice but to
reluctantly disclose Chantal's malicious scheme rather
than allow him to blunder in all unsuspecting.

That he might not accept her word had never occurred
to her, so that now, on hearing him dismiss her warning
so heedlessly, she could only stare at him, momentarily
nonplussed.

'Or are you, perhaps, just trying to keep us apart
because you were annoyed she paid me so much attention the other night?' he went on to ask suspiciously.

Ravelle's eyes opened wide in astonishment. 'Now
who's being ridiculous!' she couldn't help countering,
sardonically. 'I admit I was a trifle taken aback by her
behaviour, but that's a long way from being annoyed

enough to deliberately mislead you because of something so inconsequential.'

'Oh, I see.' Matthew's features hardened markedly. 'What you're really saying is, that you have no need to concern yourself because you don't believe other women could be attracted to me, is that it?'

'Not other women like Chantal Gregory, no, I'm afraid I don't.' Her dark brown eyes sought his pleadingly. 'Matthew, work it out for yourself! She's pretty, she's rich, and she's used to mixing with only the most influential people. Now what can you offer her that she hasn't already got, or can't find within her own social set?'

'As to that, it might surprise you to learn we have quite a lot in common,' he retorted, and obviously piqued.

'Such as . . . you both like table tennis, and you both get sunburnt?' drily.

'Amongst other things!' he snapped. 'But now, if you've quite finished being facetious, I suggest you forget the matter. All this performance over one friendly match is just too absurd.'

'You mean to go ahead with it, then, despite everything I've said?'

'Naturally!'

Ravelle gave a defeated sigh. He clearly wasn't going to let himself be dissuaded no matter what arguments she proffered. A sudden thought leapt into her brain and she tilted her head sideways, her features becoming wryly quizzical.

'Matthew, you don't by any chance *want* her to be attracted to you, do you?'

'Of—of course not!' he blustered, the guilty flush suffusing his cheeks hinting otherwise. 'You know very well I'm not the type to be unfaithful.'

'I didn't say you were,' she pointed out, not a little

ironically. 'But at the same time, you wouldn't exactly be *unhappy* at the thought of Chantal being interested in you either, now would you?'

'Garbage! You're talking absolute garbage again!' he charged angrily, but still slightly red-faced. 'The trouble with you is, you're just jealous because I'll be spending the morning with her and not with you!'

'Somehow I doubt you'll be spending much time with her at all, but don't let me stop you if you're so keen, you go right ahead,' Ravelle recommended mockingly, heading for the verandah. Once there, she turned back to face him, her soft mouth curving obliquely. 'You'll be able to find me on the beach . . . awaiting the outcome of your match with great interest.'

Matthew didn't appreciate her parting shot—as evidenced by the grated expletive he threw after her—but after she had returned to her own cabin in order to change into her bikini and collect a towel before making her way on to the beach, it still came as no shock to her to see him stomping infuriatedly across the sand in her direction only a relatively short time later.

Coming to a halt beside her, he dropped down on to a corner of her towel, his eyes wrathfully bright. 'Now I suppose you're going to gloat, "I told you so"!' he charged bitterly.

Ravelle shook her head negatively. She hadn't the slightest desire to do anything of the kind. In lieu, she probed tentatively, 'I gather Chantal did—er . . .'

'Don't ever mention that venomous bitch's name to me again!' his order slashed through her question with the sting of a whip. 'The supercilious, patronising cow! I felt like wiping the smirk off her face with the back of my hand! Do you know what she had the utter gall to say to me? Do you?' he repeated incredulously, his voice unconsciously rising.

Thankful no one was close enough to hear, she

grimaced ruefully, sympathetically. 'I think I—er—have a general idea. She more or less gave me a brief summary last night.'

Matthew cracked his knuckles, the look on his face as he did so making Ravelle wonder if he wasn't imagining the sound to be that of Chantal's neck breaking, then he heaved a loud sigh.

'I should have listened to you earlier,' he conceded, but didn't apologise for his unfounded accusations of the time, she noted. 'She wouldn't have had the opportunity to let loose with her virulent abuse if I had. Although, she won't escape retribution altogether.' His expression changed to one nearing pleasurable anticipation. 'Her sister and brother-in-law weren't too overjoyed to hear what I had to say, I can tell you.'

'You told Erin and Vance?' Ravelle's finely arched brows rose considerably higher.

'Too right I did! I wasn't having that arrogant piece talk to me like that without reporting it. Who does she think she is, anyway? Just because her sister is a part-owner in the place, that doesn't give *her* any special rights!' He glanced at Ravelle with a belligerent scowl descending on to his forehead. 'Why, don't you think I was entitled to complain about her?'

'I—well, I guess so, if you wanted to,' she shrugged. If it had been herself she would rather have kept the altercation private, but now was patently not the time to admit to such thoughts. Not while Matthew was in such a fighting mood!

Mollified by her answer, he leant back in a more relaxed position. 'At least one good thing's come out of it,' he advised enigmatically, his lips pressing into lines of complacency.

Since he didn't elucidate, Ravelle surmised she was supposed to ask, and did so in wry accents. 'Oh, and what's that?'

'This afternoon we're to be personally conducted over Hermitage on our own *private* trail ride,' he all but crowed. 'Not like that fishing trip yesterday where I was just one of a number, or the group trail ride they had us listed for, but one of our very own.' If possible the look on his face became even more smug. 'They weren't particularly anxious to go along with the idea at first, of course, but I finally convinced them it was in their best interests.'

'You mean, you used your argument with Chantal as an excuse to ask for further concessions?' she queried in distaste.

'I thought it was only right we should receive some recompense for the treatment I was subjected to,' he retorted haughtily, resentfully. 'And I didn't ask, I *demanded*! In no uncertain terms either, I might add.'

Ravelle could imagine! Probably by threatening to write to all manner of organisations in order to destroy the good reputation Erin and Vance were attempting to build for the resort, she deduced knowingly. Matthew liked writing letters, especially to the newspapers, and it was more than likely his form of exaggerated complaints could have quite a detrimental effect on a place like Morning Retreat—whether they were substantiated or not.

Having received the exact opposite to the praise he had expected, Matthew eyed her huffily. 'You might at least show some pleasure in the idea after all the trouble I went to,' he complained. 'I thought you wanted to see over Hermitage.'

As he hadn't as yet seen fit to even enquire how she had occupied herself during his absence the day before, Ravelle once again decided it was an inauspicious time for revealing the truth and conveniently forgot to tell him she had already been escorted over the island.

'Yes, naturally I do,' she concurred diplomatically instead. 'What time is our—er—tour due to start? When the tide's low enough for us to cross over?'

'Hardly!' he denounced derisively. 'If we waited that long we'd only get to see half the island before having to return for dinner. No, it's for immediately after lunch. Vance is arranging for someone to take us over in one of the runabouts.'

Ravelle pursed her lips thoughtfully. 'Don't you think a whole afternoon's riding—when neither of us has ever ridden before—may be just a little too much for a first attempt?'

'I don't see why . . . if their horses are as well-behaved as they claim. I don't envisage they'll be doing anything but walking.'

'Mmm, but even so . . .'

'For heaven's sake, Ravelle!' he cut in vexedly, stiffening. 'I arranged this ride with you in mind, and I can't see that one afternoon spent riding around at a leisurely pace is going to create any overwhelming problems, so I would appreciate it if you'd kindly stop trying to pick fault with the plan and concentrate on being a little more grateful instead!'

'All right, I'm grateful!' she flared, and rolling over on to her stomach presented her sleek bronzed back to him. 'I just thought it might make us too stiff to move for the next couple of days, that's all!'

'Even if it does, it'll be worth it.'

A subtle change in his tone had her sending him a frowning gaze over one shoulder. 'Just so you can have a privately conducted tour?' she puzzled.

'Not altogether,' he smiled—or was it smirked? She wasn't quite sure which. 'You see, I also happen to have stipulated exactly *who* is to be our guide.'

'Oh?' Her frown deepened. 'Does it matter?'

'To me it does,' he nodded emphatically. 'I thought it

would be rather appropriate if the person who so
arrogantly started all this trouble should now find himself cast in a more subservient role thanks to this latest
episode.'

Ravelle slewed around quickly to sit facing him again,
her expression a mixture of disbelief and dismay. 'You've
specified *Steele* as our guide?' she gasped.

'Mmm, I thought that would surprise you.'

Surprise her? She was closer to being dumbfounded!
Not only because he was vengeful enough to nominate
Steele, but also because he was naïve enough to think
Steele would accede. That latter assumption was almost
laughable!

'And—and what did Vance have to say about that?'
she quizzed with a gulp.

'He said his brother would be advised of my stipulation.'

'He didn't actually say Steele would definitely be
accompanying us, though?'

Matthew looked at her askance. 'That's as good as!' he
declared confidently.

Ravelle wasn't nearly so assured, but nevertheless held
her peace. In a couple of hours' time they would know
for certain which of them was correct.

In his increasingly normal fashion Matthew had a
complaint to make even before they left Hideaway. This
time because Dion had been Vance's choice to take them
across to the other island in the runabout—not a more
senior member of the staff—and as the three of them
stepped into the boat he took his seat with ill grace, fixing
the youngster with a disapproving glance.

'I hope you know how to manage this thing,' he
growled mistrustfully.

'Oh, yes,' Dion nodded as he started the motor and
swung the craft about as competently as ever. Indicating

the tiller he made as if to rise. 'But you can take over, if you like.'

Ravelle had to turn her head away in order to hide the irrepressible grin which sprang to her lips, knowing her fiancé was as ignorant of all things nautical as she was, and feeling Matthew shuffle uncomfortably beside her.

'No, you can stay there,' he allowed hastily. 'Just make sure you keep your mind on what you're doing, that's all.'

'Of course!' From the look Dion gave him in return it was plain he had never contemplated doing otherwise. The bright blue eyes were directed at Ravelle next. 'You must've really liked Hermitage yesterday to be going back again so soon,' he guessed, pleased.

Unfortunately for Ravelle she had no option but to smilingly agree—not for anything could she have hurt the child's feelings by denying him his obvious pleasure at the thought—but at the same time she couldn't repress a shiver as she waited for Matthew's inevitable comments. He didn't keep her in suspense for long!

'You came over here yesterday?' he challenged furiously, his face darkening with his anger. 'Without waiting for me?'

'Well, I—I didn't have anything in particular to do, so when Dion and his brother asked me if I'd like to see some of Hermitage, I—I thought I might as well,' she offered apologetically. 'I couldn't really see any harm in it. It's a big island and I'm sure there's still a lot more to see.'

To her unbounded relief Dion didn't contradict that statement, as she had suspected he might, but remained silently watching them with eyes a little less lively than they had been but a great deal more astute. Matthew, on the other hand, had plenty to say.

'Would you have cared if there wasn't?' he charged

sarcastically. 'No, you were obviously just thinking of yourself . . . again! You knew very well I'd planned for us to come over here together, yet the minute my back was turned you couldn't wait to sneak across and see it first. Now I can understand why you couldn't summon up any enthusiasm when I told you I'd arranged trail rides for this afternoon.' His lips thinned censoriously.

'That wasn't the reason at all,' she denied in a low mutter, annoyed that he couldn't at least have kept his reprimands until they were alone. 'It was because I thought a whole afternoon's riding might be too much. And I didn't sneak over here, I can assure you. I came quite openly. Since you had considered it was only necessary to arrange a fishing trip for *your*self, I fail to see how you can possibly complain about the way in which I chose to occupy myself!'

'And that's just why you did it, isn't it?' he sneered. 'To spite me because you didn't get a trip too!'

'Oh, don't be so ridiculous! Spite had nothing whatsoever to do with it. I went because I had nothing else planned at the time, and because Dion and Craig invited me.'

'Hmm, after a few pointed hints from you, no doubt!'

Ravelle was saved the necessity of answering—and thereby prolonging the dispute—by the boat grounding on Hermitage's white sands. Matthew immediately jumped on to the beach and began striding for the trees, leaving Dion to offer a helping hand to his remaining passenger.

'Gee, I'm sorry I got you into trouble,' he said penitently as soon as she was ashore. 'I didn't mean to.'

Shrugging, she grimaced ruefully. 'That's okay, it wasn't your fault. I'm afraid Matthew gets a little touchy at times.'

He seemed relieved she didn't blame him and his customary smile made its reappearance. 'Oh, I nearly forgot,' he grinned, one hand digging into the pocket of his shorts to bring forth a key on a small ring. 'That's for the red moke—the one we used yesterday. So you don't have to walk up to the yards.'

'Thank you.' Ravelle accepted it gratefully, raising expressive eyes skywards. 'In this heat I don't think I'd fancy . . .'

'Are you coming, or are you going to stand there whispering all afternoon?' Matthew broke in with an impatient shout.

Sighing, she smiled wryly at Dion, thanked him for bringing them over, and then hurried after her fiancé.

'We weren't whispering,' she smouldered on reaching him. 'He was giving me this,' holding up the key, 'so we could use one of the mokes. Or would you prefer to walk all the way up that damned hill?'

'There's no need to swear,' he reproved coldly. 'I should have thought it was their duty to provide transport.'

'Well, it isn't! It says in the brochure there are mokes *for hire* on Hermitage, so I thought the least I could do was to say thanks for being allowed the use of one for free.'

'Huh!' he snorted scornfully. 'If the truth were known, your thanks should probably have been given to me. I expect they knew I wouldn't let them get away with forcing us to walk up there.'

'Mmm. you could be right,' she granted acidly. 'I suppose they figured it would be cheaper to provide a moke rather than take the chance on being subjected to another dose of your blackmailing!'

'Call it what you like, but I notice you're not averse to accepting the benefits,' he jeered.

'Oh?' Ravelle halted in her tracks, eyes opening sardonically wide. 'Then that's easily rectified, seeing I was only accompanying you out of an—apparently misguided—sense of loyalty.' About-facing, she promptly started back the way they had come.

'If you think you can walk off and leave me just like that, you'd better think again!' Matthew rasped, chasing after her to grab hold of her arm and drag her around. 'I organised this ride for both of us, and you're damned well going to take part in it!'

'Not unless you apologise, I'm not!'

He stared at her wrathfully. It clearly went against the grain for him to admit having been wrong, but it was also plain he didn't want her disagreement with his actions made quite so obvious.

'All right, I apologise!' he finally snapped.

'With such sincerity too!' she gibed.

Although he didn't retaliate, the tautening of his slight frame and the threatening glitter which shone from his narrowing eyes showed just how incensed he was by her taunt, and as a consequence, Ravelle wasn't really surprised that he should totally ignore her on the drive up to the yards.

What did cause her some astonishment on the moke's arrival, however, was to see Steele—whom she just hadn't anticipated being there, Matthew's stipulation notwithstanding—calmly helping another young man to saddle four horses. Dressed almost identically in jeans, check shirts, and bush hats, the two of them finished cinching the mounts they were working on, and then waited for Ravelle and Matthew to join them.

As observant as ever, it only took Steele a moment to surmise from their demeanour that, once again, all was not well between the two approaching him, and noting the twitch of wry amusement which began pulling at his lips, Ravelle sent him a vexed glare. A look he either failed to see, or chose to disregard, for as they moved closer it was on Matthew that he focussed his gunmetal gaze.

'I see you got your brother's message.' It was Matthew who spoke first, in a discernibly gloating tone.

Ravelle waited tensely for the explosion, only to find none forthcoming as Steele clarified amiably, 'Regarding your choice of escort? Mmm. So now perhaps I'd better introduce you. Ravelle Fenton, Matthew Inglis, meet Jim Purlow . . . your guide for the afternoon.'

The eruption Ravelle had been expecting now came from Matthew, even before she'd acknowledged the other man's greeting.

'Oh, no, you're not getting away with this, Cunningham! I distinctly specified *you* for that position,' Matthew grated.

'I know,' smiled Steele aggravatingly, completely in control. 'But I'm sorry, I don't happen to be one of the employees here. I'm only on the island in an advisory capacity for the cattle breeding programme, and the men could take strong exception if they thought management was taking over their duties.'

From the bantering inflection in his voice, and the covert grin which split Jim's face, it was plain there was no such likelihood, but even so Matthew knew demarcation was a dicey subject to take lightly—no matter what the circumstances—and, as a result, his attack was reduced to a spluttering peevishness.

'But—but there's four horses saddled,' he pointed out accusingly.

'Oh, I'll be travelling a short distance with you, to ensure there are no problems . . . for Jim,' Steele drawled sardonically.

'Then why not all the way?' demanded Matthew sharply.

'Because, quite honestly, there are more important matters which require my attention elsewhere,' came the smooth rebuff. 'So, shall we get started?' And without waiting for a reply Steele caught hold of the reins on the brown-coated animal closest to him, designating, 'Ravelle?'

'Why not me?' Matthew immediately questioned suspiciously.

'Because Lady has a very soft mouth and is, first and foremost, a ladies' mount,' Steele explained drily. 'Or is that what you would prefer?'

With an uncomplimentary mutter beneath his breath, Matthew stalked across to where Jim had brought forward a slightly larger roan, leaving Ravelle to approach her mount hesitantly.

'Don't look so worried, she won't bite, I can assure you,' Steele grinned lazily and flicked a finger towards the end of her tip-tilted nose.

Ravelle smiled faintly, reluctant to admit even to herself that it was his presence causing most of her trepidation, not the horse, but more than content to let him continue thinking it was otherwise.

'Okay then, up you go.' He held the stirrup steady while she clutched at the pommel to pull herself awkwardly up and into the saddle. 'Right, now keep your knees turned in so they're in light contact, let your heels drop down . . .' He slanted her a wryly disapproving look. 'You should never ride in footwear without heels, you know.'

Glancing down at the offending pale blue sneakers which matched her slim-fitting canvas jeans, she grimaced apologetically. 'I don't have a pair of heeled shoes with me, only open sandals.'

'Mmm, not very suitable, I agree,' he conceded, and continued with his instructions. 'As I said, heels well down but relaxed, or else your legs will become as stiff as blazes, toes up and slightly outward.' His dark brows peaked enquiringly. 'How do the stirrups feel for length? Too long—too short?'

'No, they feel fine . . . so far,' she half laughed nervously.

'On to the reins, then.' To date he had been holding those, but now his beautifully shaped mouth began to tilt humorously. 'Of course you do realise you're going to have to let go of the pommel in order to hold them, don't you?' he drawled.

Fighting against the wild riot of feeling his smile induced, Ravelle flushed and unwound her clenched fingers. 'I—I was only hanging on in case she moved,' she excused selfconsciously.

'She won't—well, apart from the odd shuffle or two, maybe—but she certainly won't set off, if that's what you're afraid of. Here,' he took hold of her left hand to run the rein towards her between ring and little finger, across the palm, then forward again between her thumb and index finger. 'Now run it through your right hand the same way and let the slack just hang between the two,' he directed.

'Like this?'

'Uh-huh!' This time he folded a strong hand over hers and using a slight pressure eased Lady's head to the left, asking, 'Can you feel her mouth?'

Ravelle nodded, pleased.

'Good.' He allowed Lady's head to return to the front. 'Now you try it on the other side. That's the girl,' he commended as she followed his instructions implicitly. 'There are a few more points to turning, of course, such as leg and heel pressure, but I think you'll find she's so used to these trail rides that she'll know when to turn better than you will, and since it's your first time I reckon you'll find it easier if there's not too much to try and remember. One thing you should always keep in mind, though, is that these,' he tapped her heel, 'are your accelerators. For today, I'd recommend you make certain you use them very gently.'

Swallowing, Ravelle nodded vigorously to demonstrate her total accord. 'And—er—more importantly, I presume these,' looking down at the strips of leather threaded between her fingers, 'are the brakes.'

'Sure are,' he laughed. 'Just shorten the rein and she'll shorten stride.' Moving across to the same chestnut animal he had been riding the day before, he swung into the saddle with a lithe grace Ravelle envied after her somewhat struggling effort to do the same, and gathering the reins into one hand urged his mount alongside hers.

'How come I have to use both hands when you only use one?' she queried.

'Because, at a guess, I'd say I'm slightly more experienced than you are,' Steele smiled mockingly.

'Oh—well—I wasn't to know that, was I?' she retorted a trifle resentfully.

'That I was a more practised rider than you?' One eyebrow crooked tauntingly.

Ravelle let the caustic glare she sent him do her talking for her, and then turned to watch Matthew and his mentor. Steele's next comment promptly had her reversing the action, however.

'Seeing that Matthew arranged this ride for both of you—even though it appears you've had another of your little in-fights on the way—I assume you haven't broken your engagement to him as yet?' he probed, but quietly enough so the other two couldn't overhear.

'No, not yet,' she answered stiffly, still a little nettled by his recent goading.

He shook his head slowly, incredulously. 'God only knows why you're holding off! I know for a fact you're not overly attached to him.' His eyes rolled skywards. 'Who the hell could be to a bombastic whiner like that? Moreover, it's not even as if he treats you decently, he'd have to be the most selfish mongrel I've ever come across.'

Ravelle thought it best to neither deny nor confirm his accusations, but merely raised one shoulder non-committally. 'Well, I did sort of try yesterday afternoon,' she disclosed grudgingly.

'And?'

'He couldn't see any need to break our engagement.'

'Whereupon you told him differently, I trust!'

'Well, no, not really. You see, he w-wasn't feeling very good at the time. He'd just arrived back from his fishing trip, and—and . . .'

'So once again you allowed him to dictate conditions and thereby lost the opportunity,' he charged exasperatedly.

She began chewing dejectedly at her lip. 'Something like that, I suppose.'

Steele released a heavy breath, his expression becoming sardonic in the extreme. 'And all for a man you continually argue with!' A mirthless laugh issued from the column of his bronzed throat. 'My God, you amaze me, honey, you really do!'

Stung, she rounded on him hotly. 'So would Matthew too, probably, if you knew him as well as I do! Okay, I admit we've had more than our fair share of arguments since we've been here, but at the same time he still possesses some admirable qualities which are totally absent from your character, Steele Cunningham!'

'For example?' he bit out curtly.

As she was already rueing her impetuous attack Ravelle could have hugged Jim for his timely intervention when he elected that particular moment to advise, 'We're ready if you are,' and, consequently, diverted Steele's attention away from herself.

'Right, let's get going then,' he nodded shortly, heeling his mount into motion. 'I don't want to waste any more time than I have to.'

Suspecting that last sniping comment had been meant for herself even more than it had been for her fiancé, Ravelle sighed despondently. Now not only was she in

Matthew's bad books, but she had succeeded in riling
Steele as well!

'Are you coming or staying?'

It was Steele's voice, heavy with sarcasm, that penetrated her musings, and on looking up she found him
watching her impatiently from a few metres away.
Matthew and Jim were a little farther on, making slowly
for the meandering trail which led through a pocket of
dense rain forest situated just below the plateau.

'I'm coming,' she murmured in a subdued whisper,
and gingerly pressed her heels against Lady's sides. To her
relief the obedient mare moved forward sedately and,
as she found the movement not too unbalancing,
Ravelle's apprehension began to decrease. But only until
Steele swung his mount alongside to keep pace with her,
and then it was replaced by a nervousness of a completely
different kind as she sent him a surreptitious glance from
beneath thickly curling lashes.

'I'm sorry,' she offered forlornly on seeing the tight set
to his jaw.

'Don't worry about it, we'll catch them up,' his answer
came in clipped tones.

'Well, for that too, I guess, but I was actually referring
to—to what I said before.'

The grey gaze which came to rest on her was deliberately goading. 'You mean, you're sorry I don't have
Matthew's praiseworthy traits, or that you're just sorry
you mentioned them?'

'I mean, I just don't want to argue with you too!' she
cried distractedly.

'Matthew well and truly keeping your hands full in
that regard, huh?'

Ravelle turned her head away dispiritedly. Apparently
he was more interested in continuing his taunts than in
accepting her apology and, regretting once again the
impulsive words which had provoked him to such an

extent, she unconsciously pressed her heels to Lady's sides in order to induce a slightly faster gait. The sooner they reached Steele's point of departure, perhaps the sooner she would be able to take some pleasure from the ride instead of futilely struggling to maintain her equanimity in the face of his gibes and his disturbingly overpowering presence.

Matthew and Jim were waiting for them at the edge of the rain forest, and as the track winding through it was so narrow they were forced to proceed in single file, with Jim leading the way and pointing out the many and varied species of trees, vines, and ferns, as they went. Matthew was next, his expression indicating that he had neither forgiven Ravelle for having previously visited the island, nor become reconciled to the fact that Steele wasn't to be at his beck and call for the afternoon. Close behind him followed Ravelle—while Steele brought up the rear—and finding Lady was quite content to amble along after the others without any specific instructions from her, Ravelle was able to listen interestedly to Jim's narrative and to gaze in wonder at the thickly canopied, and dimly lit, primeval growth which surrounded them.

It was not only a fascinating sight to behold but also a somewhat awe-inspiring one as well, she found, when contemplating the thousands of years required to produce such an immense array of plant life, but unluckily, owing to her preoccupation with this new environment she didn't notice Matthew carelessly shouldering past some half dead branches from a brambly type bush which was growing at the side of the trail.

Her first intimation to beware—a roughly voiced, 'Watch it!' from Steele—had her reacting rapidly, but her reflexes still weren't quite fast enough to avoid the backswing of the branch altogether. It still managed to slap against the side of her head as she attempted to duck beneath it, and to not only tangle viciously within her hair, but also, by some freak chance, to spear through the centre of the plaited gold ring in her ear with a wrenching force that split the skin open.

With an involuntary cry, Ravelle dropped the reins from her right hand—whereupon Lady promptly came to a halt—and automatically clamped her hand to her injured ear, an action which immediately brought forth another startled exclamation of pain when she connected with the imprisoning thorns. Then Steele was gently easing his mount beside her as far as he could in order to help release her.

'Keep still, honey,' he cautioned anxiously, his lips levelling angrily as he surveyed her quite freely bleeding ear, 'or you'll just pull on it and make it worse.'

'It feels as if it's already reached its worst!' she quipped, but on a decidedly quavering note.

Up ahead, both riders had come to a stop on hearing Steele's initial warning, but although Jim now swung about, preparing to come back, Matthew merely turned in his saddle, eyeing Ravelle's predicament exasperatedly.

'Those damned earrings!' he charged irritably. 'I've told you before you're asking for trouble wearing them. And goodness only knows why you'd have them on for a trail ride!'

Steele's fingers ceased their careful manipulation and his eyes took on an icy sheen. 'Is that all you've got to say?' he had rasped before Ravelle could speak.

'What else do you expect?' Matthew returned his look haughtily. 'It's her own fault.'

'That's a matter of opinion! It was you who let the branch swing back. Or don't you believe its necessary to show your fiancée even the smallest common courtesy?' Steele enquired in disgusted tones.

'Not since I presumed she'd be looking where she was going,' retorted Matthew truculently. 'And if she wasn't—that being the reason for your warning call, I gather—then as I said, she has no one to blame but herself!'

Stifling a savage epithet, Steele inhaled a furious breath, glancing past him to where his stockman sat frowning, in amazement. 'I suggest you and *Mr* Inglis,' with unconcealed contempt, 'continue on your way, Jim,' he ground out implacably.

With an understanding nod the younger man made to comply, but not so Matthew. He recklessly remained where he was to challenge, 'I'll make the suggestions as to when we move on, Cunningham, not you! And I say we'll stay!'

'I wouldn't recommend it . . . *for your sake*!' Steele countered forebodingly, and returned his attention to Ravelle.

'Are—are you threatening me again?' came the demand, albeit somewhat warily as Matthew suddenly seemed to realise just how formidable-looking was the opponent he'd chosen for himself.

'Yes, I'm threatening you!' Steele looked up to verify grimly. 'Now get the hell out of here while you're still able, and let me concentrate on what I'm doing!'

'You can't . . .'

'Please, Matthew, you go on,' interrupted Ravelle persuasively, finally managing to get a word in for herself. 'We'll catch you up again shortly.'

'After we've returned to the house and that ear's been bathed,' added Steele adamantly.

Obviously torn between an increasingly thwarted desire to assert some dominance and a wish to continue his ride, Matthew eventually chose the latter. 'All right, I guess I may as well. There's not much point in both of us being penalised, and especially since you had no such qualms about seeing the island without me yesterday,' he declared maliciously in parting.

Ravelle merely uttered a dismal sigh, surmising it wasn't the last she would be hearing on the subject, while Steele muttered something extremely scathing under his breath and continued disentangling her from the bush. It took quite some time before the task was completed and she could move her head without feeling as if either part of her scalp or her ear was being removed, and she voiced her appreciation of his painstaking efforts in all sincerity.

'More to the point,' he dismissed her gratitude with a casual movement of broad shoulders, 'how does your ear feel?'

'Better than it did a short while ago,' she admitted thankfully, raising a tentatively assessing hand to the damaged area. Unfastening the offending piece of jewellery, she slipped it carefully out from her ear to study both it and her bloodstained fingers in surprise. 'Good heavens, I didn't realise it had bled that much.' A quick look at her shoulder showed her sleeveless top to have fared no better. 'From the mess it's made it looks as if I've had my throat cut.'

His ensuing grin was wryly formed. 'With the ability you seem to possess for riling members of the opposite sex, honey, I'm sure that's a distinct possibility for the future,' he drawled.

'It's only been happening since we've been here,' she protested a little resentfully. 'And I don't try to annoy Matthew.'

'Only me, hmm?'

Her dark glossy lashes fanned down to lie like dark smudges against her creamy cheeks. 'I was under the impression I irritated you just by being at Morning Retreat,' she divulged tonelessly.

'Mmm, perhaps you do at that,' he owned with a dry half laugh. 'Although I hardly think now is the time to discuss it. That ear badly needs cleaning up, so I suggest we direct our attention to doing just that for the time being.'

Ravelle was more than willing to agree. A verbal confrontation was the last thing she needed right at the moment and, dropping her earring into the front pocket of her jeans, she re-gathered Lady's reins and prepared to follow Steele back to the yards.

On their arrival, much to her puzzlement, instead of leaving the two animals hitched to the rails as she had anticipated him doing since she didn't expect her ear to require lengthy attention, he unsaddled both their mounts and turned them into a paddock.

'Why did you set the horses loose and put everything away? We won't be all that long, will we?' she questioned as they made their way to the last of the three houses situated amongst the trees.

'Probably not—dealing with your injuries,' he answered her last query first, even if a trifle enigmatically. 'As for the other—well . . .' a lazy smile caught at his lips, simultaneously making her heart falter and her eyes to regard him suspiciously, 'I figured I was doing you a favour.'

'Oh, in what way?'

'By saving you from the torture Matthew was willingly prepared to subject you to just so he could boast about getting something for nothing.' A strong brown hand captured her chin, tipping her face up to his. 'Believe me, honey, you're well out of it, because if he goes ahead with this grand tour he's arranged for himself, not only will he be extremely stiff and sore for the next couple of days, it's more than likely he'll be raw in a few places as well.'

Ravelle's expression clouded sympathetically. 'Poor Matthew! I did wonder if that might be the case when he told me this morning what he'd planned, only he reckoned . . .' Remembering just what Matthew had reckoned, she jerked to a flustered stop.

'Mmm?' Steele urged, eyes taunting.

'Oh, nothing.' She shrugged away from him, discomfited, and hurried up the steps on to the verandah.

He followed more slowly. 'Since I was his choice for a guide, I don't suppose it could have been anything to the effect that he didn't really care, provided it gave him the opportunity to throw some orders in my direction for a change, could it?' he speculated shrewdly, ironically.

The flood of colour which rushed into her cheeks told him all he wanted to know.

'Was that also the reason for your participation, Ravelle?' he queried, but with a rather less amused inflection.

'No!' she denied hoarsely. 'I only came along because he said—because he said he'd arranged the ride for my sake.'

'And you believed him?' It was very apparent Steele didn't. 'Knowing he's probably never had an unselfish thought in his life? I could see how considerate he is towards you in there,' nodding sharply towards the rain forest they had just left. 'It wouldn't have worried him if you'd bled to death! He wasn't even interested in offering to help you!'

'He didn't exactly have much chance to while you were ordering him to leave,' she defended.

'He would have done . . . if he hadn't been so occupied in telling you it was all your own fault.'

'Well, maybe I shouldn't have worn these particular earrings.'

'And your hair? Are you going to suggest you shouldn't have worn that either?' Dragging his hat from his head, Steele threw it on to one of the verandah chairs, then raked his fingers roughly through his own dark thatch, tousling it. 'Damn it, Ravelle, I just can't understand why you keep making excuses for the man. Surely you must be at least a little disappointed he couldn't even show some compassion? Personally, I felt like murdering him, he was so . . . uncaring!'

'I think we all realised how you felt . . . including Matthew in the end,' she half smiled faintly. 'And I do thank you for—for taking my side, as it were, and for helping me when it—it really wasn't up to you to do so. But as for being disappointed in Matthew's behaviour . . .' Pausing, she lifted one slim shoulder philosophically, her gaze not quite meeting his. 'Well, I guess the reason I'm not is because I never expect him to show any sympathy. In fact, it was quite a surprise the other night when he became so solicitous, thinking I had heat exhaustion. He's usually too concerned with his own health to have time to worry about anyone else's.'

'Then perhaps it's just as well I did decide to accompany you part of the way, after all,' Steele deliberated brusquely and, dropping a hand on to the nape of her neck, began propelling her into the house before him. 'Otherwise he probably would have expected you to continue with it as it is.'

The deepened tone in his voice had Ravelle flicking him a nasty glance. 'I wasn't angling for any pity, you know,' she asserted. 'Nor was I indulging in self-pity. I was merely stating the facts.'

'I know!' he nodded sharply. 'That's what makes it so detestable.'

From the hall he showed her into a cream and coffee-coloured tiled bathroom, where he promptly caught her about the waist and summarily sat her on the side of the large vanity unit.

'Right, now let's see what we need,' he mused as he slid open the mirror door of a recessed cabinet above the marbled basin.

Ravelle watched him covertly. 'Would you mind telling me why I have to sit up here?' she quizzed wryly.

'Because it will be easier for me to see what I'm doing,'

he replied absently, bending to retrieve a bowl from the
cupboard beneath where she was sitting, and which he
then proceeded to fill with warm water. 'Here, hold this.'
He handed it to her after adding some liquid from a
bottle he'd taken from the cabinet.

'You don't have to bathe it,' she protested. 'There's
nothing wrong with my hands. I could do it myself.'

'I doubt it. Unless, of course, you happen to be unique
in that you're able to see behind your own ears,' he
drawled, and dropped some cottonwool into the bowl.
'Now, swing your legs round the side and let me get on
with it, huh?'

Since she apparently wasn't going to be allowed any
choice in the matter, Ravelle gave a resigned sigh and
did as she was told. But although Steele went about his
ministrations as gently as possible, there were still times
when she couldn't help flinching, even though she said
nothing, and it was an extremely relieved breath she
exhaled on hearing him eventually advise, 'All finished.
You can relax now, honey.'

'Thank you,' she murmured softly. 'I'm sorry I was
such a jittery patient.'

Efficiently disposing of the items he'd used, Steele sent
her such a gently reassuring smile that the tautness which
had just been leaving her now returned threefold. 'You
were okay,' he contended indolently. 'I'm only sorry it
hurt as much as it obviously did.' His eyes crinkled
disarmingly at the corners. 'I guess I'm more used to
doctoring cattle than I am soft-skinned females.'

Ravelle flushed selfconsciously. 'Maybe so, but I still
doubt if anyone else could have been more careful, and—
and I am grateful.'

He grazed the back of his fingers across her cheek in a
softly caressing motion. 'My pleasure,' he smiled, and
bent to brush his lips lightly, comfortingly against hers.

Although it had obviously been intended as a dispassionate gesture, the tension which immediately flared between them was anything but unemotional, and when Steele lowered his head a second time to explore the trembling softness of her mouth for a longer period, scorching flames of desire raced through Ravelle, laying waste her defences.

No matter what pain he might have caused her in the past, her heart still belonged to him—would only ever belong to him—and while his arms were drawing her inexorably closer to his rugged frame and his lips were claiming hers so possessively, there was only one thing she wanted to do, could do, and that was to respond.

With a deep-felt groan Steele reluctantly lifted his head as he scooped her into his arms and turned for the door, his grey eyes dark and passionate as they locked with sultry brown.

'Dear God, there should be a law against the way you affect me!' he charged thickly.

Ravelle's eyes glowed a little deeper and her arms linked a little tighter about his neck as he carried her through to the adjoining bedroom, but she didn't reply. Words would only interrupt the flow of feeling which had been suppressed for so long, and it was with words that all their problems seemed to begin. No, she decided dreamily, now was not the time for talking, but for savouring the emotions only he could arouse.

Sinking down with her on to the bed, Steele sought the hectic pulse at the base of her throat with sensuous lips, his hands stirringly exploring the rounded curves of her pliant body as she arched to meet him. With shaking fingers Ravelle unfastened his shirt, delighting in the feel of tautly rippling muscles beneath her trailing palms, and moaning softly, pleasurably, on discovering his hands hadn't been idle either and that they now cupped bare, swelling breasts.

In a feverish haze she moved against him provo-

catively, clutching convulsively at his broad back when
his mouth marked a burning path downwards to tease
and envelop already hardening nipples, and sending such
wild sensations of ecstasy rushing to every extremity that
she didn't think it possible to survive such rapture.

If anything, Steele was a more skilful lover now than
he had been four years before. Or maybe it just seemed
that way because, having once experienced the enchant-
ment to be found in his arms, she knew in advance the
breathtaking heights of intoxication they were capable of
reaching together. But whatever the reason, her response
was as ardent, as freely given, as he could have wished,
and when his stimulating mouth returned to hers and his
hand felt for the fastening of her jeans, there was no
thought of refusal in her mind, only a corresponding
hunger for fulfilment.

That was, until the sound of voices penetrated her
consciousness, both of them stilling their movements, and
bringing her eyes flashing open in panic to hear an all too
familiar voice demand testily, 'Well, if this is the right
place, why doesn't someone answer?

Matthew! Sucking in a horrified breath, Ravelle
darted an apprehensive glance at the man beside her.

CHAPTER NINE

FOR a fleeting moment Ravelle believed Steele intended
to keep her exactly where she was, but then, to her
immeasurable relief, he cupped her chin in one hand and
dropped a last purposeful kiss on to her lips.

'To be continued,' he vowed huskily, and a grin, both
rueful and wry, tilted his mouth crookedly as he eased
away from her to begin rapidly buttoning his shirt.

Outside, Matthew could be heard quite plainly as he made a retort to whoever was with him. 'I don't care if they are private quarters, I'm going in! You said this was where they'd come.' Footsteps sounded along the hall, accompanied by a shouted, 'Cunningham! Where in hell are you, Cunningham?'

Steele thrust his shirt roughly into his pants and made for the doorway with lithe strides, giving Ravelle time to scurry from the bed and back into the bathroom. Righting her own clothing, she combed hasty fingers through her rumpled blonde hair and, after taking a few deep steadying breaths, made her own entrance into the hall.

Her eyes assessed the scene rapidly. Jim standing diffidently by the door and obviously wishing he was elsewhere; Steele adopting an indolent posture, arms folded loosely across his wide chest, eyes sardonically amused; and Matthew facing him belligerently, demanding in censorious tones to be told his fiancée's whereabouts.

'For goodness' sake, Matthew, I'm here, of course,' Ravelle answered for herself, moving up behind him. 'Where did you think I'd be?'

Swinging around, he eyed her measuringly, suspiciously. 'When no one replied to my knock on the door, I began to wonder!' he snapped, unappeased. A raking glance took in the undeniably warm glow suffusing her cheeks, the rosy fullness of her softly shaped lips, the still somewhat ruffled state of her hair. 'From the look of you, I'd say I was right to be so distrustful! Just how have you been occupying your time since you left us . . . by crawling into his bed?'

'More than likely!' spat a virulent voice from the doorway as a casually outfitted Chantal appeared unexpectedly and stormed towards them. 'It's what she's been after ever since she arrived on the island! Don't tell me you haven't noticed!' she half laughed sneeringly.

Deciding it would be to his definite advantage, Jim promptly made himself scarce. Steele, meanwhile, lost every vestige of negligence from his attitude as his hands were thrust into the back pockets of his denims and his expression hardened resolutely.

'Keep out of this, Chantal, it's none of your business!' he ordered peremptorily. 'I don't even know what you're doing over here, in any case.'

'Well, if it's good enough for these two opportunists to claim some of your time, I couldn't see why I shouldn't too,' she retorted angrily. 'After all, you are my favourite brother-in-law, darling, and families should stick together, shouldn't they? I mean, I knew what *she*'d be up to immediately I saw them head over here. I told her only the other night that I was wise to her little tricks, but unfortunately she doesn't appear to have learnt anything from it.'

'So!' Matthew's eyes narrowed to rancorous slits as they fastened on Ravelle. 'I'm not the only one who's had suspicions concerning you, eh? Perhaps you'd care to explain . . . if you can!'

'I'd be glad to—in private! Although why you're so ready to accept her word for anything after the way she treated you this morning, I don't know!' she rounded on him resentfully.

'Because they obviously coincide with my own thoughts, that's why!' He grabbed hold of her wrist in a painful grip and looked about him searchingly. 'Okay, you want somewhere private to have this out, where's the sitting room in this place? Or didn't you manage to see anything else but the bedroom?'

'That's enough, Inglis!' Steele intervened in a cold grating voice, and moving as if to bar their way to the pleasantly furnished lounge Ravelle had, as a matter of fact, espied on her way in to the house.

'But probably no more than the truth,' Chantal just had to add another mischiefmaking remark.

Matthew issued a disgusted snort and began dragging Ravelle after him once he'd seen the direction she meant to take, but when Steele deliberately positioned himself to halt their progress it was Ravelle who shook her head in veto.

'No—please,' she refused his unspoken offer of assistance anxiously, then gazed briefly over her shoulder to where Chantal was glaring venomously after them. When she turned back again it was with a studied indifference. 'It appears you also have some explaining to do,' she murmured a little caustically.

Now that her emotions were safely under control once more, and Chantal had arrived to remind her of Steele's possible commitment in that direction, shame and embarrassment were rapidly making themselves felt as Ravelle thought of her uninhibited reactions to his lovemaking. Even if he was the only man she had ever loved, surely she had more sense than to fall into the same trap that had been her downfall four years ago! Or hadn't she learnt *anything* from that experience? Steele liked to play the field—even Chantal could testify to that!—and it would be in her best interests to remember that fact instead of senselessly allowing him the opportunity to add her name twice to his undoubtedly lengthy list of casual conquests.

'Well?' Matthew's grating enquiry pierced her meditation as he slammed the sitting room door shut with a crash and pushed her furiously towards the centre of the room. 'Let's hear it! What have you got to say for yourself?'

Ravelle's head lifted defiantly. Perhaps if he'd shown a little more consideration on the trail ride none of this would have happened.

'About what?' she flared. 'How grateful I was to

Steele for attending to my ear when you so obviously couldn't have cared less?'

'That depends on just how you showed your gratitude, doesn't it?' he snarled. 'Although from the dishevelled looks of you both that isn't hard to guess!' Grasping her by the shoulders, he shook her roughly. 'I was right, wasn't I, Ravelle? You did crawl into bed with that arrogant, grey-eyed . . .' Abruptly, he stopped, the veins standing out prominently on his forehead as his face became covered with a mottled red tint. 'You bitch! You immoral, promiscuous bitch!' he slated, his hand cracking first across one of her cheeks, then back across the other, and rocking her head so hard that she would have fallen if the fingers of his left hand hadn't been digging so tightly into her shoulder. 'I knew he reminded me of someone, and now I know exactly who . . . Samara! She's got those very same secretly amused grey eyes too! She didn't come from any first marriage—if there was one,' sneering, 'did she, Ravelle? She's Cunningham's illegitimate brat, isn't she? *Isn't she?* One you were planning to foist on to me, you brazen, deceiving trollop!' He slapped her again, but with such force this time that he hurt her lip, and making her cry out involuntarily as she spun away from him to half fall across the seat of a sofa.

No sooner had she done so than the door flew open and Steele burst into the room. Sizing up the situation in a mere second, he caught hold of Matthew's shoulder to spin him around before the younger man even had time to be fully aware they had company, and then sent him reeling against the wall and thence sprawling to the floor with a backhand Ravelle was surprised didn't break his jaw.

'So you like to play rough, do you, Inglis?' he gritted between clenched teeth, a nerve beside his jaw tensing grimly as he bent to hail Matthew to his feet by his shirt front. 'Well, let's see how good you are with someone of your own sex, huh?'

Matthew came up threatening, if not fighting. 'I'll sue you for this, you interfering swine!' he ground out, though somewhat groggily. 'And don't think you've heard the last about trying to palm off your unwanted bastard and its no-good tart of a mother on to me either, because I'll be making certain everyone knows about it!' He gave a sneering half laugh. 'Then we'll see the Cunninghams cut down to size, won't we?'

'But only after I've had the pleasure of doing the same for you!' So saying, Steele sent a solid right smashing into Matthew's jaw which had him crumpling to the floor again—but unconscious this time. Bending, Steele then slung the inert form over his shoulder and left the room, heading for the front of the house.

When he returned some few minutes later Ravelle had wiped the blood from her lip and was watching the doorway with despondent eyes. 'What did you do with him?' she asked in a slightly apprehensive tone.

'Dumped him in the moke and told Jim to get him off the island before I changed my mind and broke his miserable neck, after all!'

She nodded faintly. 'And—and Chantal?'

'I told *her* much the same,' sardonically.

'I'm sorry,' she whispered penitently. If it hadn't been for Matthew and herself, he probably would have spent a congenial afternoon in the other girl's company. 'I—I'm sorry Matthew discovered Samara was your daughter too. He could make things very difficult.'

Steele eased agilely down on to his haunches in front of her and, lifting one hand, swept her hair gently back from her face. 'For you?' he quizzed softly.

A slender shoulder lifted in a non-committal gesture. 'I was thinking of Sam and—and you, actually.'

'You don't think the Cunninghams capable of dealing

with someone like Inglis, if it really becomes necessary?'
His lips twitched wryly.

Yes, she supposed her anxieties were a little misplaced
in that regard. 'I wouldn't want Sam to have to pay
for—for my mistakes, though.'

'Don't sweat, she won't!' There was nothing but
confidence in his tone. 'She'll be a Cunningham too,
remember?'

Something in her expression must have alerted him,
because he promptly ensnared her chin between thumb
and forefinger and probed shrewdly, 'You're still not
reconciled to that idea, hmm?'

Ravelle tried to avert her head, but he wouldn't let
her. 'I'll get used to it in time, I guess,' she shrugged.

'Will it be so difficult?'

'Of course!' The words flashed out swiftly, then she
sighed and looked at him with shadowed eyes. 'It's the
first step t-towards losing her c-completely, isn't it?'

'Why on earth would it be when she'll still be living
with you?' he frowned in astonishment.

'Because that's what I *feel* will happen,' she answered
tearfully. 'As she gets older she's bound to associate herself more with the person who bears the same name as she
does, isn't she?'

'Oh, honey!' With a rueful shake of his head Steele
pushed himself partly upright and on to the sofa beside
her, his hands clasping her shoulders and turning her
squarely to face him. 'That wasn't my intention in
suggesting it . . . to take her away from you.'

'You threatened to before,' she pointed out miserably.

His well-cut mouth assumed a wry shape. 'Mmm, but
as I recall, I'd only just discovered I had a daughter, and
your choice of a stepfather sure didn't tally with mine.'
He touched an evocative finger to the cut in her lip and
his features tightened drastically. 'I still feel like murdering the cowardly little rat for what he's done to you this

afternoon. In fact, the more I think about it, the more I'm inclined to regret hitting him so hard that second time. It would have afforded me considerably greater pleasure if he'd stayed on his feet longer so that I could have thrown a few more at him.'

'Yes—well—I certainly appreciated your intervention even if Matthew didn't,' Ravelle confessed with an instinctive shudder of remembrance. 'It was almost as if he lost all semblance of control when he discovered Sam was your daughter.'

'I knew I shouldn't have left you alone with him!' Steele slapped a hand down on to his thigh in a gesture of self-annoyance. 'I suspected right from the first that was more than likely the way he'd go if he was crossed.' For a moment he was silent and then his gaze became quizzical. 'What made you tell him about her, anyway?'

'I didn't—he guessed. I told you he'd already said you reminded him of someone. Well,' she spread her hands explicitly, 'this afternoon he suddenly realised just who that person was.'

'You didn't attempt to deny it?'

Ravelle half laughed humourlessly. 'I wasn't given a chance to deny or confirm it. He was too busy venting his own feelings for me to say anything at all.'

'Oh, God, I'm sorry, kitten,' he groaned, drawing her to him comfortingly. 'If I hadn't kissed you after we'd finished in the bathroom, probably none of this would have taken place.'

If he hadn't kissed her four years ago it wouldn't have either, she reflected sorrowfully, but it was impossible to say as much, because his use of that long-forgotten nickname had put a lump in her throat the size of a tennis ball and it was some time before she could speak at all. When she did, it was in as unaffected a voice as she could manage under the circumstances.

'It doesn't matter,' she asserted huskily, and pulling

slightly away from his disconcerting hold. 'I suppose it was a foregone conclusion it would happen some time, and at—at least it's broken my engagement. Well, I presume it has.' Her accompanying forced laugh quavered and died beneath the heartbreaking look stealing over his face.

'But leaves us with some unfinished business to attend to, I believe,' he claimed deeply, meaningfully, as his head inclined inexorably downwards.

For the initial few achingly sweet seconds Ravelle couldn't deny herself the delight of accepting his sensuously knowing exploration of her receptive lips, but then, and only by summoning her last reserves of willpower, she made herself remember the shame and embarrassment she had experienced as a result of her previous response and frantically dragged her mouth away from the devastating contact.

'No!' she protested jerkily, throatily.

'Why not, Ravelle?' From within their ebony frames his smoky grey eyes roved questioningly over her troubled countenance, but his arms refused to give her struggling form freedom. 'I know you want me as much as I want you.'

'No, you're wrong!' she cried desperately, and unsuccessfully trying to avoid his descending mouth before it captured hers again. 'I don't want you—I don't!'

'Liar,' he drawled lazily against the corner of her trembling lips. 'Your head may tell *you* that, but the rest of you tells *me* something entirely different.'

And how could she dispute it when her mouth was clinging to his so unreservedly, and her errant senses were departing one by one to leave her absolutely defenceless against his electrifying onslaught? There was only one recourse open to her, and she grabbed at it like a drowning man grabbing at straws.

Catching him unawares, she abruptly twisted her head

free, her breath coming in shallow, uneven gasps, 'How much will you be offering me this time?' she asked, and not a little bitterly.

Steele raised his head slowly, disbelievingly almost, the tension emanating from his stiffening figure nearly palpable and sending shivers of trepidation splintering along Ravelle's spine.

'You mercenary little . . .!' He bit off an expletive, his eyes registering his contempt as his arms fell away from her in disgust and he rose to his feet to tower over her formidably. 'There's a name for women who demand payment in return for making love—I've no doubt you're familiar with it! But just for the record, honey, although you may have been a good lay—for a virgin—I've no intention of paying twice for the same piece of goods . . . and especially not *used* goods!' he lashed at her crudely, despisingly.

Ravelle was shaking so much she could hardly get to her own feet, but her hand managed to find its mark all the same. It smacked across his cheek with a strength she hadn't realised she possessed to bring a reddening imprint surging to the surface of his bronzed skin.

'You vile, insulting animal!' she choked desolately. 'Don't you dare . . .!' She broke off with a sharp inhalation as Steele roughly gripped a handful of her hair.

'And don't you dare lift your hand to me again, or you'll discover all too quickly just what *I'm* likely to dare!' he threatened irately.

'Then don't be so damned offensive!'

His lips curled into a scornful sneer. 'Because I called a spade a spade?'

'Because you know it's nothing but a pack of lies!' she hurled back fiercely. 'You're just trying to shift the blame on to me to appease your own discomfiting feelings of guilt!'

'*My* feelings of guilt!' he repeated with an odiously

sarcastic laugh. 'You were the one who just raised the
subject of money, and if I remember correctly, I wasn't
even present last time the matter of payment came up.'

'No, that's right, you weren't, were you?' she gibed
derisively. 'In your two-faced, lily-livered fashion you
let your father do your dirty work for you!' Her eyes
widened insolently, facetiously. 'How you must miss him
now he's not here to make your filthy pay-offs on your
behalf!'

At her denunciations of double-dealing and cowardice
Steele's eyes narrowed to glacially piercing slits, and it
was obviously only thanks to a rigid self-discipline over
his escalating emotions that he was able to answer merely
with stinging mockery.

'Yeah, well, I didn't hear you making any complaints
at the time, honey. You seemed only too willing to grab
what you could and run.' The hand which was still
threaded within her hair tugged painfully, significantly.
'Or is that considered acceptable behaviour by lying,
conniving little bitches like you?'

Seething at his unwarranted disparagements, Ravelle
was nonetheless bewildered by them, and consequently
chose to continue her attack on more familiar ground.

'No, I didn't make any complaints . . . I was too
disgusted to!' she blazed hotly. 'And yes, I grabbed my
things and ran! What did you expect me to do? Wait
around in the hopes of being introduced to the fiancée
you'd conveniently forgotten to mention, but whom your
father kindly pointed out to me as you so ardently
greeted her on the wharf?'

'Not likely!' Steele scoffed. 'Not when you already
had my cheque in your hot little hand. That may have
proved too embarrassing . . . even for you!'

'And you have the unmitigated gall to censure my
behaviour!' she half laughed brokenly, incredulously.
'At least I have the comfort of being able to sleep at

night with a clear conscience knowing I didn't have hold
of it for long. I didn't want to feel contaminated!' Her
eyes met his goadingly.

'So I noticed!' he bit out witheringly. 'Although the
money it represented was something else again, I gather.'

'Meaning?' she promptly countered, suspiciously.

'You certainly weren't averse to the cash it provided
you with, though, were you? That cheque must have had
the fastest clearance through my bank of any I've ever
known!'

Ravelle gazed at him blankly, somewhat confused for
the second time now. 'I don't know what you're talking
about,' she declared with a frown. 'I didn't cash that
cheque, if that's what you're implying. I told you, I only
had hold of it for a few minutes.'

'Oh, sure!' he jeered sardonically. 'And then it just
happened to turn up in your bank account.'

'*No*! I screwed it up and threw it back at your father,
if you must know!'

'Mmm, I can imagine.' He gave a totally unbelieving
and cynical snort. 'That's the sort of thing a person does
when they've just received the payment they asked for.'

'What do you mean . . . *asked for*?' she demanded
furiously. 'You *offered* it!'

At long last Steele removed his hand from her hair—as
if he couldn't bear the contact any further. 'God, you're
willing to mouth any lie that comes into your head, aren't
you, Ravelle?' he castigated. 'But at least give me credit
for knowing when I offer something and when I don't,
because I sure as hell didn't *offer* you that damned
cheque!'

'Then—then why did your father say you had?' she
cried, more perplexed than ever.

He shrugged uninterestedly. 'I only have your
extremely doubtful word that he did. His advice to me
was completely different.'

'In other words, that I had asked for the money?' On receiving a dispassionately confirming nod, she burst out quickly, 'But that's just not true! The cheque was already made out when he brought it to my cabin. He said you had more important matters to attend to, but that you—you'd asked him to see that I received it.'

'It was made out in my handwriting?'

'Yes.'

'That's strange,' he began musingly, then fixed her with an insolently depreciating glance. 'I was informed the cheque given to you—when you called at my father's cabin to demand recompense for services rendered—was one of a number I'd already signed for some business transactions he was to fulfil on my behalf later that day, and that *he* filled in the necessary details while you waited.' One dark brow flicked satirically high. 'Another discrepancy in your story, honey? You should pay more attention to detail, because I know for a fact *I* didn't make out any cheque in your name.'

Ravelle dragged her fingers through her hair distractedly. 'Well, it looked to me as if it was in the same hand. The signature was yours, so I just assumed the printing was too.'

'Printing? My father never used printing on a cheque in his life!'

'Whether he did or not, the one he handed to me was printed,' she flared. 'Not that it matters, anyway, because I refused to accept it.'

'Ah, yes, discrepancy number two, and quite an important one, I'm sure you'll admit,' Steele mocked caustically. 'I shall be very interested to hear what story you've devised to explain how, three days after we docked, my bank balance just happened to be reduced by the exact amount of a cheque made out in your name, but which you supposedly didn't accept, and yet was deposited—I checked—to the account of one *Ravelle Fenton*!'

'Oh, God, I don't know! I just don't know!' She shook her head helplessly, her eyes beginning to blur. 'Maybe your father wanted you to think I'd taken it—he never did like me. I just wish I'd torn the damned thing up instead of throwing it back at him. He said I'd probably regret the action.'

Steele's forehead creased into a speculative frown. 'Why would he say that?'

'How should I know?' she countered despairingly. 'You knew him better than I did. You work it out!'

'Where my father was concerned, that could be a little difficult. Even at the best of times we rarely saw eye to eye.'

'Yet you're quite willing to believe every lying word he apparently told you about me,' she charged, bitterly resentful.

'Why wouldn't I?' His brows arched sardonically. 'All the evidence pointed to him being correct. In fact, it still does as far as I can see—all things considered—and especially in view of your request for another such payment only this afternoon!' He eyed her disdainfully. 'You convicted yourself with that one, honey.'

'But I wasn't asking for money!' she protested, aghast.

'It sure sounded like it to me.'

'Well, I wasn't! If anything, I was being sarcastic!' With a sigh her shoulders sagged dejectedly and her eyes sought his mistily. 'Oh, Steele, I'm not interested in your money, I never was. Why would I have asked your father, of all people, for payment? I was under the impression—however mistaken—that you wanted to marry me. Surely you can see there just wasn't any reason for me to go to him with such a request?'

He exhaled heavily, meditatively, his gaze intent as it held hers. 'However mistaken?' he curiously chose one particular point to query.

The memory was still too humiliating, even now, for

Ravelle to continue looking at him and she bowed her head to hide her anguish. 'He said—your father said—something to the effect that—that I was naïve not to realise you'd be willing to promise all sorts of things in order to—to achieve your own gratification, and that a one-night t-tumble at the end of a d-diverting voyage didn't mean much when compared to—I think he called them your f-filial ob-obligations,' she relayed chokingly.

'Then why didn't you see *me* before leaving the ship?' Steele probed on a harsh note.

'How could I? He'd already given me that cheque, which *was* signed by you, then when he said all those things and deliberately showed me you greeting your fiancée—who, until then, I hadn't even known existed!—what else was I supposed to have done? I couldn't have stood hearing you tell me the same, so I ran, as fast as I possibly could.' She paused to steady her breathing, then added, 'I figured that if, by some remote chance, it had all been some ghastly mistake then you'd contact me.' Her voice thickened deeply. 'But you never did.'

'Because, by the same token, I reasoned that if you weren't guilty, you would get in touch with me,' Steele divulged in a tone no less husky.

Despite her rising hope that his gruffness might have indicated the beginning of his, at least partial belief in her story, Ravelle still had some suspicions of her own that troubled her, and she aired them tentatively.

'H-how could you have intended marrying me when you were—were already engaged, Steele? And why,' she hurried on to the perhaps most painful query while she still had the courage to continue, 'was it necessary to tell your father we—we'd spent that last night t-together?'

'I didn't!' His denial came swiftly and succinctly. 'I thought you had. But in any case, not being told was never a barrier to him discovering what he wanted to know. He was nothing if not ruthlessly thorough in that regard. As for the other—well . . .' he hunched one muscled shoulder—uncomfortably? 'I didn't tell you because I was—oh, what the hell!—because I wasn't prepared to take the chance on losing you!' he admitted savagely. 'Kathleen's and my engagement was more of a business arrangement, I suppose you might say. I wasn't in love with her and I don't really believe she was in love with me, but since our families had expected us to marry—and at the time neither of us had any interests elsewhere—we decided we might as well tie the knot,' an oblique curve edged across his lips, 'if only to gain some relief from the family pressure that was being exerted. After I met you I knew there was no way I'd be going through with it, so I didn't tell you because I intended calling it to a halt at the very first opportunity.'

'It didn't look as if that's what you intended from the way you greeted her,' she couldn't help accusing.

'Perhaps you ought to take the credit for that,' he half laughed unexpectedly. 'After the night we'd just spent, I rather think I was imagining it was someone else entirely I was kissing.'

A warm becoming flush covered Ravelle's cheeks and she dropped her gaze selfconsciously. 'I wish I'd known,' she whispered sadly.

'Hmm, but it's all water under the bridge now.'

He made it sound as if it didn't really matter to him, one way or the other, and she chewed at her lip to disguise its sudden quivering. 'You do believe me though, don't you, that I gave that cheque back to your father?' she asked with apprehensive urgency.

'There is still that account in your name where the money was deposited,' he shrugged, not committing himself.

'I see.' It was impossible to continue hiding her despair now and she turned away from him swiftly. 'Well, I guess there's not much else I can say, is there? I can't prove I didn't take it, and you refuse to believe I didn't, although I'm expected to believe you neither wrote the cheque, nor offered it! A rather one-sided arrangement, to my way of thinking,' she went on compulsively, 'but not one I have any control over, it seems. If I had that much money I'd give it to you, just to try and prove I never wanted it in the first place—your father said you knew the advantages of a healthy bank account—but I haven't got it, so I can't. In fact . . .' A stifled sound behind her had her breaking off and automatically shooting an enquiring look over her shoulder, to find Steele shaking his head ruefully and a widening smile sweeping his firm mouth upwards.

'You find it amusing that I should want to prove my innocence, do you?' she rounded on him indignantly.

'I find it amusing when you claim there's not much else to say . . . then never stop talking,' he corrected lazily.

'Oh—well . . .'

'And for your information, honey,' he interrupted in the same drawling accents, 'whether you had that amount of money or not, I wouldn't accept it from you. No matter what you may think, it wasn't the money that was important to me, although I would like to know just how that particular remark concerning my bank account supposedly came into the conversation.'

'There's nothing "supposed" about it, it did come into the conversation!' she declared emphatically. 'It was after I'd thrown the cheque back at him. He picked it up and put it in his pocket, and that's when he said I might have cause to regret such a foolishly impulsive act of grandstanding, although you weren't likely to complain because *you* knew the advantages of a healthy bank account, even if I didn't. Then he left.'

Steele digested the information thoughtfully. 'Well, I'd have to say those are so patently the kind of comments he would make in such a situation that you couldn't possibly have invented them,' he allowed finally.

'Then you do believe I'm telling the truth, after all?'

'I do believe it's time I set some enquiries in motion regarding the signature of the Ravelle Fenton who deposited that cheque,' was as far as he would relent.

'You didn't before?' she queried, her surprise momentarily overcoming her disappointment.

'Until now it hadn't appeared necessary.'

Ravelle couldn't entirely agree, but the thought that he was about to at least try and get to the bottom of the matter was enough to give her spirits a lift. 'But you do think it's possible to uncover that signature?'

Metallic grey eyes locked closely with soft shining brown. 'You're positive you want me to?'

'Naturally I . . .' Abruptly she stopped as the implication of his query sank in. Then she exploded in a smouldering fury. 'You snake! I'm wasting my time trying to convince you, aren't I? because you just don't *want* to believe me! Well, from now on I don't give a damn whether you do or not, and to hell with you, Steele Cunningham!' For the second time that afternoon she sent a hand winging furiously towards his face.

Only on this occasion it was halted before it found its target, by a lean inflexible hand which promptly twisted her arm behind her back at the same time as it hauled her close to his virile frame. It all took place with such paralysing alacrity there wasn't an opportunity for her to protest against, or resist, the lips which proceeded to possess hers with the same mesmerising despatch until quite some minutes later.

'Wh-what do you think you're doing?' were her first stunned words when he eventually raised his head.

'Don't you know?' he teased drily, his arms continuing to keep her pinned against him.

Ravelle refused to find any humour in the situation.

'All right then . . . why?' she demanded hotly.

'Because I love you—have always loved you—will always love you.' A rueful smile tugged at the corners of his mouth. 'Those reasons enough?'

'But—but . . .' Finding her arms free, Ravelle immediately flung them around his neck, discarding her attempts to seek elucidation in favour of taking things in their order of importance. '*Oh, yes!*' she sighed ecstatically. 'Oh, yes!'

Not surprisingly, it was a response that brought forth an extremely fervent, extremely welcome reaction, and when Steele lifted her on to the sofa, cradling her in his strong arms, her lips continued to cling to his in blissful adoration until he at last, reluctantly, broke away.

'This time I don't intend letting you out of my sight until after I've got you to the altar,' he vowed with a heartfelt groan. 'We've wasted too many years already.'

She smiled upwards lovingly, banteringly. 'Do I take that to be another offer of marriage?'

'I guess that depends on whether you think another one's necessary,' he grinned back indolently. 'To my knowledge, I've never retracted the last offer I made.'

Ravelle cupped his face tenderly within slim fingers. 'Then, since I've never withdrawn my acceptance either, I think I'd prefer to let our original agreement stand.' For a moment she was contentedly silent, but there were other questions she wanted answered, and finally she could withhold them no longer. 'Steele, what made you change your mind?' she quizzed curiously. 'I was so certain you never would when you queried if I really wanted you to discover that signature.'

'Mmm, so I gathered,' he smiled wryly. His arms tightened about her instinctively. 'And I'm sorry I had to ask it, but . . .' his expression turned regretful, 'in view of the fact that there were so many differences between your account of what happened and the one I'd been given, I was forced to use what little means were available in order to distinguish which one was the truth.'

'You were testing me?'

'I'm sorry,' he apologised again. 'But if you'd shown even the merest hint of unwillingness, or wariness . . .' He allowed the sentence to trail away meaningfully.

'I didn't, though, did I?' she was able to beam happily.

'Deep down I don't think I really believed you would, although at the same time I wasn't expecting quite such a violent reaction either!' With an enchanting smile he eyed her mock-threateningly. 'You're going to have to curb that disconcerting habit you seem to have acquired of letting fly with your right hand, kitten.'

Her return grin was irrepressible. 'Oh, I think I can safely promise it won't happen again. It was just something I picked up from Matthew this afternoon.' She slanted him a glance full of mischief. 'But effective, wouldn't you say?'

'Too damned effective!' he agreed, wryly devout. Touching her cheek with the tips of his fingers, he sucked in a sharp breath. 'I can imagine what it must have felt like for you when that snivelling . . .!' He broke off tautly, shaking his head. 'I'd still like to break his neck for daring to lay a hand on you!'

Ravelle was willing to be a little more forgiving. After all, Matthew's behaviour had partly been responsible for her present state of happiness.

'But then you never did like him, did you?' she put forward reflectively.'

'That's an understatement!' Steele half laughed ironically. 'You'd be somewhere closer to the truth if you said I've hated his guts from the moment I first saw him!'

'Because he tried to have you turned out of the dining room?'

'Because you were engaged to him!' A self-mocking smile made an appearance. 'Initially I might have kidded myself into believing it was anger at you that I was transferring to him, but in actual fact it was just a case of old-fashioned jealousy because you were with him and not me.'

'So you set about dropping all those nasty innuendoes to make him suspicious of our relationship,' she glowered.

'Uh-huh!' he smiled impenitently. 'Since you'd walked out on me—as I thought—and I'd broken my engagement because if I couldn't have you I just didn't want anyone else, then I figured it would only be what you deserved if I made things as uncomfortable as possible for you. Then when Matthew kindly told me the date of,' he bent to kiss her softly, '*our* daughter's birthday . . .'

'You immediately threatened to take her away from me!' she interposed with a hurt look.

'I know, I know,' he sighed contritely. 'But could you really blame me? The thought of that pompous little upstart rearing a child of mine was just intolerable! God, I still can't understand what made you even become engaged to him!'

'Oh, there were a number of reasons that seemed reasonable at the time,' she smiled a little sadly. 'Probably because he was the exact opposite of you, being the most important. It's been hard enough having Sam reminding me every time I look at her without taking on a husband who might, however unwittingly, do the same in some way.'

'Why contemplate marriage at all, then?'

She hunched one shoulder helplessly. 'I was lonely, I suppose, and at least while I was with Matthew my thoughts weren't continually returning to the past and wishing for what might have been.'

Steele rested his chin on the top of her head, his fingers stroking over her hair soothingly. 'It's been a lot harder for you than it has for me, hasn't it, kitten?' he murmured sympathetically. 'I'm afraid it just didn't occur to me you might become pregnant because of our last night together.'

Tilting her head back, Ravelle laid a kiss to the side of his jaw. 'It didn't to me either until a couple of months later,' she chuckled wryly. 'And by then, there wasn't much I could do about it.'

'You never considered having an abortion?' heavily.

'Oh, no!' She shook her head vehemently. 'Not only was the baby a part of me, but also my last remaining link with you, and—subconsciously, anyway—I think I wanted that most of all.'

'Lord, what a fool I was to have taken my father's word for what happened!' he berated himself angrily. 'I didn't at first—I accused him of lying—because I just couldn't believe I'd been so wrong about you.'

'That's how I felt too, but apparently he was very adept at playing both ends against the middle.'

'Mmm, I should have remembered that was a favourite ploy of his,' Steele ground out bitterly. 'He clinched many a business deal by just that tactic, the remorseless old . . .'

'No, don't say it!' Ravelle sealed his lips with her fingers. 'He was your father, in spite of everything, and he'll never be able to come between us again. Besides, he probably thought he was doing it in your best interests.'

'The company's best interests, don't you mean?' he contradicted drily. 'Believe me, he would have gained considerably from my marriage to Kathleen Maynard.'

'Kathleen *Maynard*! Is that who you were engaged to?' Her eyes rounded incredulously. 'No wonder he wanted me out of the picture! The Maynards are heavily into iron ore, aren't they?'

His affirmation came in the form of a wry inclination of his head.

'Oh, Steele!' She gazed at him adoringly as she twined her slender arms about his neck once more and began pulling his head down to hers. 'I do love you so!'

Perfectly willing to oblige, he claimed her inviting mouth. When he finally relinquished it again, it was to drawl deeply, 'Not that I'm complaining, mind you, but just how did that happen to come into the conversation at this particular time?'

She grinned impishly. 'Because I felt like it, and,' her face sobered slightly, 'because you chose me in preference to someone like Kathleen Maynard.'

'I'd choose you in preference to anyone, my love, because I only feel half alive without you,' Steele owned huskily.

With a contented sigh she nestled closer to his muscular form and flicked him a teasing glance from beneath long thick lashes. 'You didn't seem to feel that way when you kissed me on my first night here.'

'Didn't I?' he countered, humorously dry. 'Why else do you think I was so rough on you in the beginning? Because I discovered all too quickly that as far as I was concerned nothing had changed. I still wanted you as much as ever, yet all you appeared to care about was finding excuses for Matthew! Everything he did, you defended, and in my resentful state that was like waving a red rag at a bull. So that was when I decided to change my strategy and seek my revenge in less obvious ways.'

'Oh?' she half smiled, half frowned. 'I don't know that I like the sound of that.'

Steele started to laugh, a sound like deep velvet that filled her with warmth. 'Don't worry, all I succeeded in doing was deceiving myself. Unfortunately for me, every scheme I tried—from trying to part Matthew from you, you from Matthew, to making you fall in love with me again—all had the same vital flaw. Somewhere along the line in each of them I had the idea in the back of my mind that I was going to finish by making love to you, and for a plan of revenge I could tell that was going to be somewhat self-defeating,' he smiled ruefully.

'And was all what h-happened between us this afternoon before Matthew arrived j-just a part of your r-revenge?' she faltered. The idea that it might have been had the power to hurt unbearably.

'Oh, no, honey, that was something quite spontaneous,' he reassured her earnestly. 'I didn't even have any intention of kissing you, except that you'd had such a rotten time of it I couldn't help myself. What followed was just a natural progression because of the way I feel about you—it's only ever been you I've wanted in my arms—and you can take my word for it, there certainly wasn't anything calculated in my actions.'

'I'm glad, because it's only your arms I've ever wanted to be in,' Ravelle confessed a trifle shyly in her relief. 'That's why I had to ask how much you were planning to offer me when you started kissing me again after Matthew had gone. I could feel myself giving in and I was desperate to find something to stop you.'

'But why? That's what I couldn't make out, and partly the reason I said such callously hurtful things to you afterwards.'

Diverted for the moment, she caught her bottom lip between her teeth. 'Do you really think of me as—as used goods, Steele?' she asked, but not without an uncontrollable wince. 'I—I've never been to bed with anyone else, you know.'

'Oh, God!' He shook his head despairingly. 'Of course I don't think of you like that, and I apologise for being so insensitive as to suggest it. All I can offer in my own defence—as little consolation as it may be—is that I just wasn't prepared either for your words, or the feelings of hostility they brought swarming back.'

'At—at least it cleared the air between us.'

'One would surely hope there were more pleasant ways of doing it, though,' wryly.

'I suppose so, but I had to find some way to stop you. I was terrified of having my scalp added to your collection of casual conquests twice.'

'I can see your point,' Steele conceded drily, 'although there was certainly no danger of you ever becoming a conquest—casual or otherwise. Where you're concerned, I have the distinct feeling I'm the one who surrenders!'

'That could be a handy piece of information for the future,' she dared to tease, and was rewarded by a looked of feigned menace. 'Although after what Chantal had to say the other night, I . . .'

'Oh? And just why would she be having something to say?' he cut in intently.

Ravelle's winged brows peaked in surprise. 'Well, I—I presumed . . . You mean, she hasn't been your girl-friend?'

'Not bloody likely!' His reply was nothing if not straight to the point. 'Whatever—or should I say, who-ever?—gave you that idea? Chantal?'

'I—I thought that was what she implied. I must have misunderstood her,' she offered excusingly.

'I doubt it,' he half laughed wryly. 'Chantal can be good company at times, but she has the aggravating habit of thinking the man who can resist her hasn't been born yet.'

'She doesn't mean anything to you, then?'

'As a romantic interest?' He shook his head slowly, the warmth she could see in his eyes telling her all too clearly just where his interests in that direction lay. 'No, I've escorted her around a few times, but there's never been anything to it on my part. Besides, she's too anxious to possess a man, body *and* soul, for my liking.'

'What if I said *I* felt that way . . . about you?' she enquired throatily. Where this man was concerned she suspected that was exactly how she did feel.

'Hmm.' Lazy grey eyes surveyed her measuringly, and then he smiled so captivatingly that she thought her heart would break. 'Then for you, I guess I'd have to make an exception, wouldn't I?'

She couldn't ask for more, she could only repay, and the first of many willing instalments was made then and there.

Harlequin Plus

A WORD ABOUT THE AUTHOR

Although for many years she has considered herself an Australian, Kerry Allyne was in fact born in England. Her early childhood was uneventful, she remembers, until her father came home one day and began talking about emigrating to Australia. When they eventually arrived in Australia Kerry took to her new land with a passion.

During the family's first years "down under," she explored as much of the country as she could, journeying northward into Queensland and out onto the Great Barrier Reef, and sometimes south through New South Wales into Victoria. "Always there was something new to see and experience."

These youthful travels were to be tucked away until the time came when Kerry began writing in earnest. But first she returned to England for a working holiday. Then, back in Australia, she met her husband-to-be, an engineer.

After marriage and the birth of two children, the family headed north to Summerland—a popular surfing resort, where today they run a small cattle farm and an electrical-contracting business.

When her youngest child started school, Kerry Allyne decided to fill her days by writing a novel. Her attempt was entitled *Summer Rainfall* and was published in 1976 as Romance #2019. "Following the doubts that accompanied its mailing," she says, "the thrill of having it accepted was totally unbelievable!"

Kerry Allyne says that rural Australia is a great source of inspiration for a writer—"one that gives me great enjoyment to try to capture on paper."

Readers of Kerry's Romances will agree that she has succeeded admirably in this task!

Take these **4** best-selling novels **FREE**

ANNE HAMPSON
gates of steel

ANNE MATHER
sweet revenge

VIOLET WINSPEAR
devil in a silver room

JANET DAILEY
no quarter asked

Harlequin Presents...

Take these
4 best-selling novels
FREE

 *The very finest
in romantic fiction*

Get all the latest books before they're sold out!

As a Harlequin subscriber you actually receive your
personal copies of the latest Presents novels immediately
after they come off the press, so you're sure of getting all
8 each month.

Cancel your subscription whenever you wish!

You don't have to buy any minimum number of books.
Whenever you decide to stop your subscription just let us
know and we'll cancel all further shipments.

**Your
FREE gift
includes**

Sweet Revenge by **Anne Mather**
Devil in a Silver Room by **Violet Winspear**
Gates of Steel by **Anne Hampson**
No Quarter Asked by **Janet Dailey**